Virgins

Diana Gabaldon is the author of the international bestselling Outlandernovels and Lord John Grey series.

She says that the Outlander series started by accident: 'I decided to write a novel for practice in order to learn what it took to write a novel, and to decide whether I really wanted to do it for real. I did – and here we all are trying to decide what to call books that nobody can describe, but that fortunately most people seem to enjoy.'

And enjoy them they do – in their millions, all over the world. Published in 42 countries and 38 languages, in 2014 the Outlander novels were made into an acclaimed TV series starring Sam Heughan as Jamie Fraser and Caitriona Balfe as Claire. Seasons three and four are currently in production.

Diana lives with her husband and dogs in Scottsdale, Arizona, and is currently at work on her ninth Outlander novel.

Also available by Diana Gabaldon

OUTLANDER SERIES

Outlander (previously published as Cross Stitch)

Claire Randall leaves her husband for an afternoon walk in the Highlands, passes through a circle of standing stones and finds herself in Jacobite Scotland, pursued by danger and forcibly married to another man – a young Scots warrior named Jamie Fraser.

Dragonfly in Amber

For twenty years Claire Randall has kept the secrets of an ancient battle and her daughter's heritage. But the dead don't sleep, and the time for silence is long past.

Voyager

Jamie Fraser died on the battlefield of Culloden – or did he? Claire seeks through the darkness of time for the man who once was her soul – and might be once again.

Drums of Autumn

How far will a daughter go, to save the life of a father she's never known?

The Fiery Cross

The North Carolina backcountry is burning and the long fuse of rebellion is lit. Jamie Fraser is a born leader of men – but a passionate husband and father as well. How much will such a man sacrifice for freedom?

A Breath of Snow and Ashes

1772, and three years hence, the shot heard round the world will be fired. But will Jamie, Claire, and the Frasers of Fraser's Ridge be still alive to hear it?

An Echo in the Bone

Jamie Fraser is an 18th-century Highlander, and ex-Jacobite traitor, and a reluctant rebel. His wife, Claire Randall Fraser, is a surgeon – from the 20th century. What she knows of the future compels him to fight; what she doesn't know may kill them both.

Written in My Own Heart's Blood

Jamie Fraser returns from a watery grave to discover that his best friend has married his wife, his illegitimate son has discovered (to his horror) who his father really is, and his nephew wants to marry a Quaker. The Frasers can only be thankful that their daughter and her family are safe in 20th-century Scotland. Or not . . .

DIANA GABALDON

VIRGINS

CENTURY

1 3 5 7 9 10 8 6 4 2

Century
20 Vauxhall Bridge Road
London SW1V 2SA

Century is part of the Penguin Random House group of companies
whose addresses can be found at global.penguinrandomhouse.com.

Penguin
Random House
UK

First published in Great Britain by Cornerstone Digital in 2016

www.penguin.co.uk

A CIP catalogue record for this book is available from the British Library

ISBN 9781780896618

Set in 13.5/16 pt Centaur MT
Typeset by Jouve (UK), Milton Keynes
Printed and bound by Clays Ltd, St Ives plc

Penguin Random House is committed to a sustainable future
for our business, our readers and our planet. This book is made
from Forest Stewardship Council® certified paper.

MIX
Paper from
responsible sources
FSC® C018179

Ian Murray knew from the moment he saw his best friend's face that something terrible had happened. The fact that he was seeing Jamie Fraser's face at all was evidence enough of that, never mind the look of the man.

Jamie was standing by the armorer's wagon, his arms full of the bits and pieces Armand had just given him, white as milk and swaying back and forth like a reed on Loch Awe. Ian reached him in three paces and took him by the arm before he could fall over.

'Ian.' Jamie looked so relieved at seeing him that Ian thought he might break into tears. 'God, Ian.'

Ian seized Jamie in embrace, and felt him stiffen and draw in his breath at the same instant he felt the bandages beneath Jamie's shirt.

'Jesus!' he began, startled, but then coughed and said, 'Jesus, man, it's good to see ye.' He patted Jamie's back gently and let go. 'Ye'll need a bit to eat, aye? Come on, then.'

Plainly they couldn't talk now, but he gave Jamie a quick private nod, took half the equipment from him, and then led him to the fire, to be introduced to the others.

Jamie'd picked a good time of day to turn up, Ian thought. Everyone was tired, but happy to sit down, looking forward to their supper and the daily ration of whatever was going in the way of drink. Ready for the possibilities a new fish offered for entertainment, but without the energy to include the more physical sorts of entertainment.

'That's Big Georges over there,' Ian said, dropping Jamie's gear and gesturing toward the far side of the fire. 'Next to him, the wee fellow wi' the warts is Juanito; doesna speak much French and nay English at all.'

'Do any of them speak English?' Jamie likewise dropped his gear, and sat heavily on his bedroll, tucking his kilt absently down between his knees. His eyes flicked round the circle, and he nodded, half-smiling in a shy sort of way.

'I do.' The captain leaned past the man next to him, extending a hand to Jamie. 'I'm *le capitaine* – Richard D'Eglise. You'll call me Captain. You look big enough to be useful – your friend says your name is Fraser?'

'Jamie Fraser, aye.' Ian was pleased to see that Jamie knew to meet the captain's eye square, and had summoned the strength to return the hand-shake with due force.

'Know what to do with a sword?'

'I do. And a bow, forbye.' Jamie glanced at the unstrung bow by his feet, and the short-handled ax beside it. 'Havena had much to do wi' an ax before, save chopping wood.'

'That's good,' one of the other men put in, in French. 'That's what you'll use it for.' Several of the others laughed, indicating that they at least understood English, whether they chose to speak it or not.

'Did I join a troop of soldiers, then, or charcoal-burners?' Jamie asked, raising one brow. He said that in French – very good French, with a faint Parisian accent – and a number of eyes widened. Ian bent his head to hide a smile, in spite of his anxiety. The wean might be about to fall face-first into the fire, but nobody – save maybe Ian – was going to know it, if it killed him.

Ian *did* know it, though, and kept a covert eye on

Jamie, pushing bread into his hand so the others wouldn't see it shake, sitting close enough to catch him if he should in fact pass out. The light was fading into gray now, and the clouds hung low and soft, pink-bellied. Going to rain, likely, by the morning. He saw Jamie close his eyes, just for an instant, saw his throat move as he swallowed, and felt the trembling of Jamie's thigh, near his own.

What the devil's happened? he thought in anguish. *Why are ye here?*

It wasn't until everyone had settled for the night that Ian got an answer.

'I'll lay out your gear,' he whispered to Jamie, rising. 'You stay by the fire that wee bit longer – rest a bit, aye?' The firelight cast a ruddy glow on Jamie's face, but he thought his friend was likely still white as a sheet; he hadn't eaten much.

Coming back, he saw the dark spots on the back of Jamie's shirt, blotches where fresh blood had seeped through the bandages. The sight filled him with fury, as well as fear. He'd seen such things; the wean had been flogged. Badly, and recently. *Who? How?*

'Come on, then,' he said roughly, and bending, got an arm under Jamie's and got him to his feet and away from the fire and the other men. He was alarmed to feel the clamminess of Jamie's hand and hear his shallow breath.

'What?' he demanded, the moment they were out of earshot. 'What happened?'

Jamie sat down abruptly.

'I thought one joined a band of mercenaries because they didna ask ye questions.'

Ian gave him the snort this statement deserved, and was relieved to hear a breath of laughter in return.

'Eejit,' he said. 'D'ye need a dram? I've got a bottle in my sack.'

'Wouldna come amiss,' Jamie murmured. They were camped at the edge of a wee village, and D'Eglise had arranged for the use of a byre or two, but it wasn't cold out, and most of the men had chosen to sleep by the fire or in the field. Ian had put their gear down a little distance away, and with the possibility of rain in mind, under the shelter of a plane tree that stood at the side of a field.

Ian uncorked the bottle of whisky – it wasn't good, but it *was* whisky – and held it under his friend's nose. When Jamie reached for it, though, he pulled it away.

'Not a sip do ye get until ye tell me,' he said. 'And ye tell me *now, a charaidh.*'

Jamie sat hunched, a pale blur on the ground, silent. When the words came at last, they were spoken

5

so softly that Ian thought for an instant he hadn't really heard them.

'My faither's dead.'

He tried to believe he *hadn't* heard, but his heart had; it froze in his chest.

'Oh, Jesus,' he whispered. 'Oh, God, Jamie.' He was on his knees then, holding Jamie's head fierce against his shoulder, trying not to touch his hurt back. His thoughts were in confusion, but one thing was clear to him – Brian Fraser's death hadn't been a natural one. If it had, Jamie would be at Lallybroch. Not here, and not in this state.

'Who?' he said hoarsely, relaxing his grip a little. 'Who killed him?'

More silence, then Jamie gulped air with a sound like fabric being ripped.

'I did,' he said, and began to cry, shaking with silent, tearing sobs.

It took some time to winkle the details out of Jamie – and no wonder, Ian thought. He wouldn't want to talk about such things, either, or to remember them. The English dragoons who'd come to Lallybroch to loot and plunder, who'd taken Jamie away with them when he'd fought them. And what they'd done to him then, at Fort William.

'A hundred lashes?' he said in disbelief and horror. 'For protecting your *home*?'

'Only sixty, the first time.' Jamie wiped his nose on his sleeve. 'For escaping.'

'The *first* ti – Jesus, God, man! What . . . how . . .'

'Would ye let go my arm, Ian? I've got enough bruises, I dinna need anymore.' Jamie gave a small, shaky laugh, and Ian hastily let go, but wasn't about to let himself be distracted.

'Why?' he said, low and angry. Jamie wiped his nose again, sniffing, but his voice was steadier.

'It was my fault,' he said. 'It – what I said before. About my . . .' He had to stop and swallow, but went on, hurrying to get the words out before they could bite him in a tender place. 'I spoke chough to the commander. At the garrison, ken. He – well, it's nay matter. It was what I said to him made him flog me again, and Da – he – he'd come. To Fort William, to try to get me released, but he couldn't, and he – he was there, when they . . . did it.'

Ian could tell from the thicker sound of his voice that Jamie was weeping again but trying not to, and he put a hand on the wean's knee and gripped it, not too hard, just so as Jamie would ken he was there, listening.

Jamie took a deep, deep breath and got the rest out.

'It was . . . hard. I didna call out, or let them see I was scairt, but I couldna keep my feet. Halfway through it, I fell into the post, just — just hangin' from the ropes, ken, wi' the blood . . . runnin' down my legs. They thought for a bit that I'd died — and Da must ha' thought so, too. They told me he put his hand to his head just then, and made a wee noise and then . . . he fell down. An apoplexy, they said.'

'Mary, Mother o' God, have mercy on us,' Ian said. 'He — died right there?'

'I dinna ken was he dead when they picked him up or if he lived a bit after that.' Jamie's voice was desolate. 'I didna ken a thing about it; no one told me until days later, when Uncle Dougal got me away.' He coughed, and wiped the sleeve across his face again. 'Ian . . . would ye let go my knee?'

'No,' Ian said softly, though he did indeed take his hand away. Only so he could gather Jamie gently into his arms, though. 'No. I willna let go, Jamie. Bide. Just . . . bide.'

Jamie woke dry-mouthed, thick-headed, and with his eyes half swollen shut by midgie-bites. It was also raining, a fine, wet mist coming down through the leaves above him. For all that, he felt better than he had in the last two weeks, though he didn't at once recall why that was — or where he was.

'Here.' A piece of half-charred bread rubbed with

garlic was shoved under his nose. He sat up and grabbed it.

Ian. The sight of his friend gave him an anchor, and the food in his belly another. He chewed slower now, looking about. Men were rising, stumbling off for a piss, making low rumbling noises, rubbing their heads and yawning.

'Where are we?' he asked. Ian gave him a look.

'How the devil did ye find us, if ye dinna ken where ye are?'

'Murtagh brought me,' he muttered. The bread turned to glue in his mouth as memory came back; he couldn't swallow, and spat out the half-chewed bit. Now he remembered it all, and wished he didn't. 'He found the band, but then left; said it would look better if I came in on my own.'

His godfather had said, in fact, *'The Murray lad will take care of ye now. Stay wi' him, mind — dinna come back to Scotland. Dinna come back, d'ye hear me?'* He'd heard. Didn't mean he meant to listen.

'Oh, aye. I wondered how ye'd managed to walk this far.' Ian cast a worried look at the far side of the camp, where a pair of sturdy horses was being brought to the traces of a canvas-covered wagon. *'Can* ye walk, d'ye think?'

'Of course. I'm fine.' Jamie spoke crossly, and Ian gave him the look again, even more slit-eyed than the last.

'Aye, right,' he said, in tones of rank disbelief.

'Well. We're maybe twenty miles from Bordeaux; that's where we're going. We're takin' the wagon yon to a Jewish money-lender there.'

'Is it full of money, then?' Jamie glanced at the heavy wagon, interested.

'No,' Ian said. 'There's a wee chest, verra heavy so it's maybe gold, and there are a few bags that clink and might be silver, but most of it's rugs.'

'Rugs?' He looked at Ian in amazement. 'What sort of rugs?'

Ian shrugged.

'Couldna say. Juanito says they're Turkey rugs and verra valuable, but I dinna ken that he knows. He's Jewish, too,' Ian added, as an afterthought. 'Jews are –' he made an equivocal gesture, palm flattened. 'But they dinna really hunt them in France, or exile them anymore, and the captain says they dinna even arrest them, so long as they keep quiet.'

'And go on lending money to men in the government,' Jamie said cynically. Ian looked at him, surprised, and Jamie gave him the *I went to the Universite' in Paris and ken more than you do* smart-arse look, fairly sure that Ian wouldn't thump him, seeing he was hurt.

Ian looked tempted, but had learned enough merely to give Jamie back the *I'm older than you and ye ken well ye havena sense enough to come in out of the rain, so dinna be trying it on* look instead. Jamie laughed, feeling better.

'Aye, right,' he said, bending forward. 'Is my shirt verra bloody?'

Ian nodded, buckling his sword belt. Jamie sighed and picked up the leather jerkin the armorer had given him. It would rub, but he wasn't wanting to attract attention.

He managed. The troop kept up a decent pace, but it wasn't anything to trouble a Highlander accustomed to hill-walking and running down the odd deer. True, he grew a bit light-headed now and then, and sometimes his heart raced and waves of heat ran over him – but he didn't stagger any more than a few of the men who'd drunk too much for breakfast.

He barely noticed the countryside, but was conscious of Ian striding along beside him, and took pains now and then to glance at his friend and nod, in order to relieve Ian's worried expression. The two of them were close to the wagon, mostly because he didn't want to draw attention by lagging at the back of the troop, but also because he and Ian were taller than the rest by a head or more, with a stride that eclipsed the others, and he felt a small bit of pride in that. It didn't occur to him that possibly the others didn't *want* to be near the wagon.

The first inkling of trouble was a shout from the

driver. Jamie had been trudging along, eyes half-closed, concentrating on putting one foot ahead of the other, but a bellow of alarm and a sudden loud *bang!* jerked him to attention. A horseman charged out of the trees near the road, slewed to a halt and fired his second pistol at the driver.

'What –' Jamie reached for the sword at his belt, half-fuddled but starting forward; the horses were neighing and flinging themselves against the traces, the driver cursing and on his feet, hauling on the reins. Several of the mercenaries ran toward the horseman, who drew his own sword and rode through them, slashing recklessly from side to side. Ian seized Jamie's arm, though, and jerked him round.

'Not there! The back!' He followed Ian at the run, and sure enough, there was the captain on his horse at the back of the troop, in the middle of a melee, a dozen strangers laying about with clubs and blades, all shouting.

'*Caisteal DHOON!*' Ian bellowed, and swung his sword over his head and flat down on the head of an attacker. It hit the man a glancing blow, but he staggered and fell to his knees, where Big Georges seized him by the hair and kneed him viciously in the face.

'*Caisteal DHOON!*' Jamie shouted as loud as he could, and Ian turned his head for an instant, a big grin flashing.

It was a bit like a cattle raid, but lasting longer. Not a matter of hit hard and get away; he'd never been a defender before and found it heavy going. Still, the attackers were outnumbered, and began to give way, some glancing over their shoulders, plainly thinking of running back into the wood.

They began to do just that, and Jamie stood panting, dripping sweat, his sword a hundredweight in his hand. He straightened, though, and caught the flash of movement from the corner of his eye.

'Dhooon!' he shouted, and broke into a lumbering, gasping run. Another group of men had appeared near the wagon and were pulling the driver's body quietly down from its seat, while one of their number grabbed at the lunging horses' bridles, pulling their heads down. Two more had got the canvas loose and were dragging out a long rolled cylinder, one of the rugs, he supposed.

He reached them in time to grab another man trying to mount the wagon, yanking him clumsily back onto the road. The man twisted, falling, and came to his feet like a cat, knife in hand. The blade flashed, bounced off the leather of his jerkin and cut upward, an inch from his face. Jamie squirmed back, off-balance, narrowly keeping his feet, and two more of the bastards charged him.

'On your right, man!' Ian's voice came sudden at his shoulder, and without a moment's hesitation, he turned to take care of the man to his left, hearing Ian's grunt of effort as he laid about himself.

Then something changed; he couldn't tell what, but the fight was suddenly over. The attackers melted away, leaving one or two of their number lying in the road.

The driver wasn't dead; Jamie saw him roll half over, an arm across his face. Then he himself was sitting in the dust, black spots dancing before his eyes. Ian bent over him, panting, hands braced on his knees. Sweat dripped from his chin, making dark spots in the dust that mingled with the buzzing spots that darkened Jamie's vision.

'All . . . right?' Ian asked.

He opened his mouth to say yes, but the roaring in his ears drowned it out, and the spots merged suddenly into a solid sheet of black.

He woke to find a priest kneeling over him, intoning the Lord's prayer in Latin. Not stopping, the priest took up a little bottle and poured oil into the palm of one hand, then dipped his thumb into the puddle and made a swift sign of the Cross on Jamie's forehead.

'I'm no dead, aye?' Jamie said, then repeated this information in French. The priest leaned closer, squinting near-sightedly.

'Dying?' he asked.

'Not that, either.' The priest made a small, disgusted sound, but went ahead and made crosses on the palms of Jamie's hands, his eyelids and his lips.

'*Ego te absolvo*,' he said, making a final quick sign of the Cross over Jamie's supine form. 'Just in case you've killed anyone.' Then he rose swiftly to his feet and disappeared behind the wagon in a flurry of dark robes.

'All right, are ye?' Ian reached down a hand and hauled him into a sitting position.

'Aye, more or less. Who was that?' He nodded in the direction of the recent priest.

'*Pere* Renault. This is a verra well-equipped outfit,' Ian said, boosting him to his feet. 'We've got our own priest, to shrive us before battle and give us Extreme Unction after.'

'I noticed. A bit over-eager, is he no?'

'He's blind as a bat,' Ian said, glancing over his shoulder to be sure the priest wasn't close enough to hear. 'Likely thinks better safe than sorry, aye?'

'D'ye have a surgeon, too?' Jamie asked, glancing at the two attackers who had fallen. The bodies had been pulled to the side of the road; one was clearly dead, but the other was beginning to stir and moan.

'Ah,' Ian said thoughtfully. 'That would be the priest, as well.'

'So if I'm wounded in battle, I'd best try to die of it, is that what ye're sayin'?'

'I am. Come on, let's find some water.'

They found a rock-lined irrigation ditch running between two fields, a little way off the road. Ian pulled Jamie into the shade of a tree, and rummaging in his rucksack, found a spare shirt, which he shoved into his friend's hands.

'Put it on,' he said, low-voiced. 'Ye can wash yours out; they'll think the blood on it's from the fightin'.' Jamie looked surprised, but grateful, and with a nod, skimmed out of the leather jerkin and peeled the sweaty, stained shirt gingerly off his back. Ian grimaced; the bandages were filthy and coming loose, save where they stuck to Jamie's skin, crusted black with old blood and dried pus.

'Shall I pull them off?' he muttered in Jamie's ear. 'I'll do it fast.'

Jamie arched his back in refusal, shaking his head.

'Nay, it'll bleed more if ye do.' There wasn't time to argue; several more of the men were coming. Jamie ducked hurriedly into the clean shirt and knelt to splash water on his face.

'Hey, Scotsman!' Alexandre called to Jamie. 'What's that you two were shouting at each other?'

He put his hands to his mouth and hooted, 'GOOOOOON!' in a deep, echoing voice that made the others laugh.

'Have ye never heard a war-cry before?' Jamie asked, shaking his head at such ignorance. 'Ye shout it in battle, to call your kin and your clan to your side.'

'Does it mean anything?' Petit Phillipe asked, interested.

'Aye, more or less,' Ian said. 'Castle Dhuni's the dwelling place of the chieftain of the Frasers of Lovat. *Caisteal Dhuin* is what ye call it in the *Gaidhlig* — that's our own tongue.'

'And that's our clan,' Jamie clarified. 'Clan Fraser, but there's more than one branch, and each one will have its own war-cry, and its own motto.' He pulled his shirt out of the cold water and wrung it out; the bloodstains were still visible, but faint brown marks now, Ian saw with approval. Then he saw Jamie's mouth opening to say more.

Don't say it! he thought, but as usual, Jamie wasn't reading his mind, and Ian closed his eyes in resignation, knowing what was coming.

'Our clan motto's in French, though,' Jamie said, with a small air of pride. '*Je suis prest.*'

It meant 'I am ready,' and was, as Ian had foreseen, greeted with gales of laughter, and a number of crude speculations as to just what the young Scots might be ready for. The men were in good humor from the fight, and it went on for a bit. Ian shrugged and smiled, but he could see Jamie's ears turning red.

'Where's the rest of your queue, Georges?' Petit Phillipe demanded, seeing Big Georges shaking off after a piss. 'Someone trim it for you?'

'Your wife bit it off,' Georges replied, in a tranquil tone indicating that this was common badinage. 'Mouth like a sucking pig, that one. And a *cramouille* like a – '

This resulted in a further scatter of abuse, but it was clear from the sidelong glances that it was mostly performance for the benefit of the two Scots. Ian ignored it. Jamie had gone squiggle-eyed; Ian wasn't sure his friend had ever heard the word 'cramouille' before, but he likely figured what it meant.

Before he could get them in more trouble, though, the conversation by the stream was stopped dead by a strangled scream beyond the scrim of trees that hid them from the roadside.

'The prisoner,' Alexandre murmured, after a moment.

Ian knelt by Jamie, water dripping from his cupped hands. He knew what was happening; it curdled his wame. He let the water fall and wiped his hands on his thighs.

'The captain,' he said softly to Jamie. 'He'll . . . need to know who they were. Where they came from.'

'Aye.' Jamie's lips pressed tight at the sound of muted voices, the sudden meaty smack of flesh and a loud grunt. 'I know.' He splashed water fiercely into his face.

The jokes had stopped. There was little conversation now, though Alexandre and Josef-from-Alsace began a random argument, speaking loudly, trying to drown out the noises from the road. Most of the men finished their washing and drinking in silence and sat hunched in the shade, shoulders pulled in.

'*Pere* Renault!' The captain's voice rose, calling for the priest. *Pere* Renault had been performing his own ablutions a discreet distance from the men, but rose at this summons, wiping his face on the hem of his robe. He crossed himself and headed for the road, but on the way, paused by Ian and motioned toward his drinking cup.

'May I borrow this from you, my son? Only for a moment.'

'Aye, of course, Father,' Ian said, baffled. The priest nodded, bent to scoop up a cup of water, and went on his way. Jamie looked after him, then at Ian, brows raised.

'They saw he's a Jew,' Juanito said nearby, very quietly. 'They want to baptize him first.' He knelt by the water, fists curled tight against his thighs.

Hot as the air was, Ian felt a spear of ice run right through his chest. He stood up fast, and made as though to follow the priest, but Big Georges snaked out a hand and caught him by the shoulder.

'Leave it,' he said. He spoke quietly, too, but his fingers dug hard into Ian's flesh. He didn't pull away, but stayed standing, holding Georges's eyes. He felt Jamie make a brief, convulsive movement, but said, 'No!' under his breath, and Jamie stopped.

They could hear French cursing from the road, mingled with *Pere* Renault's voice. '*In nomine Patris, et Filii* . . .' Then struggling, spluttering and shouting, the prisoner, the Captain and Mathieu, and even the priest all using such language as made Jamie blink. Ian might have laughed, if not for the sense of dread that froze every man by the water.

'No!' shouted the prisoner, his voice rising above the others, anger lost in terror. 'No, please! I told you all I –' There was a small sound, a hollow noise like a melon being kicked in, and the voice stopped.

'Thrifty, our captain,' Big George said, under his breath. 'Why waste a bullet?' He took his hand off Ian's shoulder, shook his head, and knelt down to wash his hands.

There was a ghastly silence under the trees. From the road, they could hear low voices – the Captain and big Mathieu speaking to each other, and over that,

Pere Renault repeating, '*In nomine Patris, et Filii . . .*', but in a very different tone. Ian saw the hairs on Jamie's arms rise and he rubbed the palms of his hands against his kilt, maybe feeling a slick from the chrism oil still there.

Jamie plainly couldn't stand to listen, and turned to Big Georges at random.

'Queue?' he said with a raised brow. 'That what ye call it in these parts, is it?'

Big Georges managed a crooked smile.

'And what do you call it? In your tongue?'

'*Bot*,' Ian said, shrugging. There were other words, but he wasn't about to try one like *clipeachd* on them.

'Mostly just cock,' Jamie said, shrugging too.

'Or "penis," if ye want to be all English about it,' Ian chimed in.

Several of the men were listening now, willing to join in any sort of conversation to get away from the echo of the last scream, still hanging in the air like fog.

'Ha,' Jamie said. 'Penis isna even an English word, ye wee ignoramus. It's Latin. And even in Latin, it doesna mean a man's closest companion – it means "tail."'

Ian gave him a long, slow look.

'Tail, is it? So ye canna even tell the difference between your cock and your arse, and ye're preachin' to me about *Latin*?'

The men roared. Jamie's face flamed up instantly, and Ian laughed and gave him a good nudge with his shoulder. Jamie snorted, but elbowed Ian back, and laughed too, reluctantly.

'Aye, all right, then.' He looked abashed; he didn't usually throw his education in Ian's face. Ian didn't hold it against him; he'd floundered for a bit, too, his first days with the company, and that was the sort of thing you did, trying to get your feet under you by making a point of what you were good at. But if Jamie tried rubbing Mathieu's or Big Georges's face in his Latin and Greek, he'd be proving himself with his fists, and fast, too. Right this minute, he didn't look as though he could fight a rabbit and win.

The renewed murmur of conversation, subdued as it was, dried up at once with the appearance of Mathieu through the trees. Mathieu was a big man, though broad rather than tall, with a face like a mad boar and a character to match. Nobody called him 'Pig-face' *to* his face.

'You, cheese-rind — go bury that turd,' he said to Jamie, adding with a narrowing of red-rimmed eyes, 'Far back in the wood. And go before I put a boot in your arse. Move!'

Jamie got up — slowly — eyes fixed on Mathieu with a look Ian didn't care for. He came up quick beside Jamie and gripped him by the arm.

'I'll help,' he said. 'Come on.'

'Why do they want this one buried?' Jamie muttered to Ian. 'Giving him a *Christian* burial?' He drove one of the trenching spades Armand had lent them into the soft leaf-mold with a violence that would have told Ian just how churned up his friend was, if he hadn't known already.

'Ye kent it's no a verra civilized life, *a charaid*,' Ian said. He didn't feel any better about it himself, after all, and spoke sharp. 'Not like the *Universite*'.'

The blood flamed up Jamie's neck like tinder taking fire, and Ian held out a palm, in hopes of quelling him. He didn't want a fight, and Jamie couldn't stand one.

'We're burying him because D'Eglise thinks his friends might come back to look for him, and it's better they don't see what was done to him, aye? Ye can see by looking that the other fellow was just killed fightin'. Business is one thing; revenge is another.'

Jamie's jaw worked for a bit, but gradually the hot flush faded and his clench on the shovel loosened.

'Aye,' he muttered, and resumed digging. The sweat was running down his neck in minutes, and he was breathing hard. Ian nudged him out of the way with an elbow and finished the digging. Silent, they took the dead man by the oxters and ankles and dragged him into the shallow pit.

'D'ye think D'Eglise found out anything?' Jamie asked, as they scattered matted chunks of old leaves over the raw earth.

'I hope so,' Ian replied, eyes on his work. 'I wouldna like to think they did that for nothing.'

He straightened up and they stood awkwardly for a moment, not quite looking at each other. It seemed wrong to leave a grave, even that of a stranger and a Jew, without a word of prayer. But it seemed worse to say a Christian prayer over the man – more insult than blessing, in the circumstances.

At last Jamie grimaced, and bending, dug about under the leaves, coming out with two small stones. He gave one to Ian, and one after the other, they squatted and placed the stones together atop the grave. It wasn't much of a cairn, but it was something.

It wasn't the Captain's way to make explanations, or to give more than brief, explicit orders to his men. He had come back into camp at evening, his face dark and his lips pressed tight. But three other men had heard the interrogation of the Jewish stranger, and by the usual metaphysical processes that happen around campfires, everyone in the troop knew by the next morning what he had said.

'Ephraim bar-Sefer,' Ian said to Jamie, who had come back late to the fire after going off quietly to wash his shirt out again. 'That was his name.' Ian was a bit worrit about the wean. His wounds weren't healing as they should, and the way he'd passed out … He'd a fever now; Ian could feel the heat coming off his skin, but he shivered now and then, though the night wasn't bitter.

'Is it better to know that?' Jamie asked bleakly.

'We can pray for him by name,' Ian pointed out. 'That's better, is it not?'

Jamie wrinkled up his brow, but after a moment, nodded.

'Aye, it is. What else did he say, then?'

Ian rolled his eyes. Ephraim bar-Sefer had confessed that the band of attackers were professional thieves, mostly Jews, who —

'Jews?' Jamie interrupted. 'Jewish *bandits*?' For some reason, the thought struck him as funny, but Ian didn't laugh.

'Why not?' he asked briefly, and went on without waiting for an answer. The men gained advance knowledge of valuable shipments and made a practice of lying in wait, to ambush and rob.

'It's mostly other Jews they rob, so there's nay much danger of being pursued by the French army or a local judge.'

'Oh. And the advance knowledge — that's easier come by too, I suppose, if the folk they rob are Jews. Jews live close by each other in groups,' he explained, seeing the look of surprise on Ian's face. 'They all read and write, though, and they write letters all the time; there's a good bit of information passed to and fro between the groups. Wouldna be that hard to learn who the money-lenders and merchants are and intercept their correspondence, would it?'

'Maybe not,' Ian said, giving Jamie a look of respect. 'Bar-Sefer said they got notice from someone – he didna ken who it was, himself – who kent a great deal about valuables comin' and goin'. The person who knew wasna one of their group, though; it was someone outside, who got a percentage o' the proceeds.'

That, however, was the total of the information bar-Sefer had divulged. He wouldn't give up the names of any of his associates – D'Eglise didn't care so much about that – and had died stubbornly insisting that he knew nothing of future robberies planned.

'D'ye think it might ha' been one of ours?' Jamie asked, low-voiced.

'One of – oh, our Jews, ye mean?' Ian frowned at the thought. There were three Spanish Jews in D'Eglise's band: Juanito, Big Georges, and Raoul, but all three were good men, and fairly popular with their fellows. 'I doubt it. All three o' them fought like fiends. When I noticed,' he added fairly.

'What I want to know is how the thieves got away wi' that rug,' Jamie said reflectively. 'Must have weighed what, ten stone?'

'At least that,' Ian assured him, flexing his shoulders at the memory. 'I helped load the wretched things. I supposed they must have had a wagon some-where nearby, for their booty. Why?'

'Well, but . . . *rugs*? Who steals rugs? Even valuable ones. And if they kent ahead of time that we were comin', presumably they kent what we carried.'

'Ye're forgettin' the gold and silver,' Ian reminded him. 'It was in the front of the wagon, under the rugs. They had to pull the rugs out to get at it.'

'Mmphm.' Jamie looked vaguely dissatisfied – and it was true that the bandits had gone to the trouble to carry the rug away with them. But there was nothing to be gained by more discussion and when Ian said he was for bed, he came along without argument.

They settled down in a nest of long yellow grass, wrapped in their plaids, but Ian didn't sleep at once. He was bruised and tired, but the excitements of the day were still with him, and he lay looking up at the stars for some time, remembering some things and trying hard to forget others – like the look of Ephraim bar-Sefer's head. Maybe Jamie was right and it was better not to have kent his right name.

He forced his mind into other paths, succeeding to the extent that he was surprised when Jamie moved suddenly, cursing under his breath as the movement hurt him.

'Have ye ever done it?' Ian asked suddenly.

There was a small rustle as Jamie hitched himself into a more comfortable position.

'Have I ever done what?' he asked. His voice sounded that wee bit hoarse, but none so bad. 'Killed anyone? No.'

'Nay, lain wi' a lass.'

'Oh, that.'

'Aye, *that*. Gowk.' Ian rolled toward Jamie and aimed a feint toward his middle. Despite the darkness, Jamie caught his wrist before the blow landed.

'Have you?'

'Oh, ye haven't, then.' Ian detached the grip without difficulty. 'I thought ye'd be up to your ears in whores and poetesses in Paris.'

'Poetesses?' Jamie was beginning to sound amused. 'What makes ye think women write poetry? Or that a woman that writes poetry would be wanton?'

'Well, o' course they are. Everybody kens that. The words get into their heads and drive them mad, and they go looking for the first man who —'

'Ye've bedded a poetess?' Jamie's fist struck him lightly in the middle of the chest. 'Does your mam ken that?'

'Dinna be telling my mam anything about poetesses,' Ian said firmly. 'No, but Big Georges did, and he told everyone about her. A woman he met in Marseilles. He has a book of her poetry, and read some out.'

'Any good?'

'How would I ken? There was a good bit o'

swooning and swellin' and bursting goin' on, but it seemed to be to do wi' flowers, mostly. There was a good wee bit about a bumblebee, though, doin' the business wi' a sunflower. Pokin' it, I mean. With its snout.'

There was a momentary silence as Jamie absorbed the mental picture.

'Maybe it sounds better in French,' he said.

'I'll help ye,' Ian said suddenly, in a tone that was serious to the bone.

'Help me . . . ?'

'Help ye kill this Captain Randall.'

He lay silent for a moment, feeling his chest go tight.

'Jesus, Ian,' he said, very softly. He lay for several minutes, eyes fixed on the shadowy tree roots that lay near his face.

'No,' he said at last. 'Ye can't. I need ye to do something else for me, Ian. I need ye to go home.'

'Home? What –'

'I need ye to go home and take care of Lallybroch – and my sister. I – I canna go. Not yet.' He bit his lower lip hard.

'Ye've got tenants and friends enough, there,' Ian protested. 'Ye need me here, man. I'm no leavin' ye alone, aye? When ye go back, we'll go together.' And he turned over in his plaid with an air of finality.

Jamie lay with his eyes tight closed, ignoring the singing and conversation near the fire, the beauty of the night sky over him, and the nagging pain in his back. He should perhaps be praying for the soul of the dead Jew, but he had no time for that just now. He was trying to find his father.

Brian Fraser's soul must still exist, and he was positive that his father was in heaven. But surely there must be some way to reach him, to sense him. When first Jamie had left home, to foster with Dougal at Beannachd, he'd been lonely and homesick, but Da had told him he would be, and not to trouble over-much about it.

'Ye think of me, Jamie, and Jenny and Lallybroch. Ye'll not see us, but we'll be here nonetheless, and thinking of you. Look up at night, and see the stars, and ken we see them too.'

He opened his eyes a slit, but the stars swam, their brightness blurred. He squeezed his eyes shut again and felt the warm glide of a single tear down his temple. He couldn't think about Jenny. Or Lally-broch. The homesickness at Dougal's had stopped. The strangeness when he went to Paris had eased. This wouldn't stop, but he'd have to go on living anyway.

Where are ye, Da? He thought in anguish. *Da, I'm sorry!*

⁓

He prayed as he walked next day, making his way doggedly from one Hail Mary to the next, using his fingers to count the Rosary. For a time, it kept him from thinking and gave him a little peace. But eventually the slippery thoughts came stealing back, memories in small flashes, quick as sun on water. Some he fought off – Captain Randall's voice, playful as he took the cat in hand – the fearful prickle of the hairs on his body in the cold wind when he took his shirt off – the surgeon's *'I see he's made a mess of you, boy . . .'*.

But some memories he seized, no matter how painful they were. The feel of his Da's hands, hard on his arms, holding him steady. The guards had been taking him somewhere, he didn't recall and it didn't matter, just suddenly his Da was there before him, in the yard of the prison, and he'd stepped forward fast when he saw Jamie, a look of joy and eagerness on his face, this blasted into shock the next moment, when he saw what they'd done to him.

'Are ye bad hurt, Jamie?'

'No, Da, I'll be all right.'

For a minute, he had been. So heartened by seeing his father, sure it would all come right – and then he'd remembered Jenny, taking yon ***crochaire* into the house, sacrificing herself for —

He cut that one off short, too, saying 'Hail Mary, full of grace, the Lord is with thee!' savagely out loud, to the startlement of Petit Phillippe, who was scuttling along beside him on his short bandy legs. 'Blessed art thou amongst women,' Phillippe chimed in obligingly. 'Pray for us sinners, now and at the hour of our death, amen!'

'Hail Mary,' said *Pere* Renault's deep voice behind him, taking it up, and within seconds seven or eight of them were saying it, marching solemnly to the rhythm, and then a few more . . . Jamie himself fell silent, unnoticed. But he felt the wall of prayer a barricade between himself and the wicked sly thoughts, and closing his eyes briefly, felt his father walk beside him, and Brian Fraser's last kiss soft as the wind on his cheek.

They reached Bordeaux just before sunset, and D'Eglise took the wagon off with a small guard, leaving the other men free to explore the delights of the city — though such exploration was somewhat constrained by the fact that they hadn't yet been paid. They'd get their money after the goods were delivered next day.

Ian, who'd been in Bordeaux before, led the way to a large, noisy tavern with drinkable wine and large portions.

'The barmaids are pretty, too,' he observed, watching one of these creatures wend her way deftly through a crowd of groping hands.

'Is it a brothel upstairs?' Jamie asked, out of curiosity, having heard a few stories.

'I dinna ken,' Ian said, with what sounded like regret, though Jamie was almost sure he'd never been to a brothel, out of a mixture of penury and fear of catching the pox. 'D'ye want to go and find out, later?'

Jamie hesitated.

'I – well. No, I dinna think so.' He turned his face toward Ian and spoke very quietly. 'I promised Da I wouldna go wi' whores, when I went to Paris. And now . . . I couldna do it without . . . thinkin' of him, ken?'

Ian nodded, his face showing as much relief as disappointment.

'Time enough another day,' he said philosophically, and signaled for another jug. The barmaid didn't see him, though, and Jamie snaked out a long arm and tugged at her apron. She whirled, scowling, but seeing Jamie's face, wearing its best blue-eyed smile, chose to smile back and take the order.

Several other men from D'Eglise's band were in the tavern, and this byplay didn't pass unnoticed.

Juanito, at a nearby table, glanced at Jamie, raised a derisive eyebrow, then said something to Raoul in the Jewish sort of Spanish they called Ladino; both men laughed.

'You know what causes warts, friend?' Jamie said pleasantly – in Biblical Hebrew. 'Demons inside a man, trying to emerge through the skin.' He spoke slowly enough that Ian could follow this, and Ian in turn broke out laughing – as much at the looks on the two Jews' faces as at Jamie's remark.

Juanito's lumpy face darkened, but Raoul looked sharply at Ian, first at his face, then, deliberately, at his crotch. Ian shook his head, still grinning, and Raoul shrugged but returned the smile, then took Juanito by the arm, tugging him off in the direction of the back room, where dicing was to be found.

'What did you say to him?' the barmaid asked, glancing after the departing pair, then looking back wide-eyed at Jamie. 'And what tongue did you say it in?'

Jamie was glad to have the wide brown eyes to gaze into; it was causing his neck considerable strain to keep his head from tilting farther down in order to gaze into her décolletage. The charming hollow between her breasts drew the eye . . .

'Oh, nothing but a little *bonhomie*,' he said, grinning down at her. 'I said it in Hebrew.' He wanted to impress her, and he did, but not the way he'd meant to. Her half-smile vanished, and she edged back a little.

'Oh,' she said. 'Your pardon, sir, I'm needed . . .' and with a vaguely apologetic flip of the hand, she vanished into the throng of customers, pitcher in hand.

'Eejit,' Ian said, coming up beside him. 'What did ye tell her that for? Now she thinks ye're a Jew.'

Jamie's mouth fell open in shock. 'What, me? How, then?' he demanded, looking down at himself. He'd meant his Highland dress, but Ian looked critically at him and shook his head.

'Ye've got the lang neb and the red hair,' he pointed out. 'Half the Spanish Jews I've seen look like that, and some of them are a good size, too. For all yon lass kens, ye stole the plaid off somebody ye killed.'

Jamie felt more nonplussed than affronted. Rather hurt, too.

'Well, what if I was a Jew?' he demanded. 'Why should it matter? I wasna askin' for her hand in marriage, was I? I was only talkin' to her, for God's sake!'

Ian gave him that annoyingly tolerant look. He shouldn't mind, he knew; he'd lorded it over Ian often enough about things he kent and Ian didn't. He did mind, though; the borrowed shirt was too small and chafed him under the arms and his wrists stuck out, bony and raw-looking. He didn't look like a Jew, but he looked like a gowk and he knew it. It made him cross-grained.

'Most o' the Frenchwomen – the Christian ones, I mean – dinna like to go wi' Jews. Not because they're

Christ-killers, but because of their . . . um . . .' he glanced down, with a discreet gesture at Jamie's crotch. 'They think it looks funny.'

'It doesna look *that* different.'

'It does.'

'Well, aye, when it's . . . but when it's – I mean, if it's in a state that a lassie would be lookin' at it, it isna . . .' He saw Ian opening his mouth to ask just how he happened to know what an erect, circumcised cock looked like. 'Forget it,' he said brusquely, and pushed past his friend. 'Let's be goin' down the street.'

At dawn, the band gathered at the inn where D'Eglise and the wagon waited, ready to escort it through the streets to its destination – a warehouse on the banks of the Garonne. Jamie saw that the Captain had changed into his finest clothes, plumed hat and all, and so had the four men – among the biggest in the band – who had guarded the wagon during the night. They were all armed to the teeth, and Jamie wondered whether this was only to make a good show, or whether D'Eglise intended to have them stand behind him while he explained why the shipment was one rug short, to discourage complaint from the merchant receiving the shipment.

He was enjoying the walk through the city, though

keeping a sharp eye out as he'd been instructed, against the possibility of ambush from alleys, or thieves dropping from a roof or balcony onto the wagon. He thought the latter possibility remote, but dutifully looked up now and then. Upon lowering his eyes from one of these inspections, he found that the Captain had dropped back, and was now pacing beside him on his big gray gelding.

'Juanito says you speak Hebrew,' D'Eglise said, looking down at him as though he'd suddenly sprouted horns. 'Is this true?'

'Aye,' he said cautiously. 'Though it's more I can read the Bible in Hebrew — a bit — there not bein' so many Jews in the Highlands to converse with.' There had been a few in Paris, but he knew better than to talk about the Universite and the study of philosophers like Maimonides. They'd scrag him before supper.

The captain grunted, but didn't look displeased. He rode for a time in silence, but kept his horse to a walk, pacing at Jamie's side. This made Jamie nervous, and after a few moments, impulse made him jerk his head to the rear and say, 'Ian can, too. Read Hebrew, I mean.'

D'Eglise looked down at him, startled, and glanced back. Ian was clearly visible, as he stood a head taller than the three men with whom he was conversing as he walked.

'Will wonders never cease?' the captain said, as though to himself. But he nudged his horse into a trot and left Jamie in the dust.

It wasn't until the next afternoon that this conversation returned to bite Jamie in the arse. They'd delivered the rugs and the gold and silver to the warehouse on the river, D'Eglise had received his payment, and consequently, the men were scattered down the length of an *allee'* that boasted cheap eating and drinking establishments, many of these with a room above or behind where a man could spend his money in other ways.

Neither Jamie nor Ian said anything further regarding the subject of brothels, but Jamie found his mind returning to the pretty barmaid. He had his own shirt on now, and had half a mind to find his way back and tell her he wasn't a Jew.

He had no idea what she might do with that information, though, and the tavern was clear on the other side of the city.

'Think we'll have another job soon?' he asked idly, as much to break Ian's silence as to escape from his own thoughts. There had been talk around the fire about the prospects; evidently there were no good wars at the moment, though it was rumored that the

King of Prussia was beginning to gather men in
Silesia.

'I hope so,' Ian muttered. 'Canna bear hangin'
about.' He drummed long fingers on the table-top. 'I
need to be movin'.'

'That why ye left Scotland, is it?' He was only
making conversation, and was surprised to see Ian
dart him a wary glance.

'Didna want to farm, wasna much else to do. I
make good money here. *And* I mostly send it home.'

'Still, I dinna imagine your Da was pleased.' Ian
was the only son; Auld John was probably still livid,
though he hadn't said much in Jamie's hearing during
the brief time he'd been home, before the redcoats –

'My sister's marrit. Her husband can manage,
if . . .' Ian lapsed into a moody silence.

Before Jamie could decided whether to prod Ian or
not, the Captain appeared beside their table, surpris-
ing them both.

D'Eglise stood for a moment, considering them.
Finally he sighed and said, 'All right. The two of you,
come with me.'

Ian shoved the rest of his bread and cheese into his
mouth and rose, chewing. Jamie was about to do likewise when the captain frowned at him.

'Is your shirt clean?'

He felt the blood rise in his cheeks. It was the closest
anyone had come to mentioning his back, and it was

too close. Most of the wounds had crusted over long since, but the worst ones were still infected; they broke open with the chafing of the bandages or if he bent too suddenly. He'd had to rinse his shirt almost every night – it was constantly damp and that didn't help – and he knew fine that the whole band knew, but nobody'd spoken of it.

'It is,' he replied shortly, and drew himself up to his full height, staring down at D'Eglise, who merely said, 'Good, then. Come on.'

The new potential client was a physician named Dr Hasdi; reputed to be a person of great influence among the Jews of Bordeaux. The last client had made the introduction, so apparently D'Eglise had managed to smooth over the matter of the missing rug.

Dr Hasdi's house was discreetly tucked away in a decent but modest side-street, behind a stuccoed wall and locked gates. Ian rang the bell, and a man dressed like a gardener promptly appeared to let them in, gesturing them up the walk to the front door. Evidently, they were expected.

'They don't flaunt their wealth, the Jews,' D'Eglise murmured out of the side of his mouth to Jamie. 'But they have it.'

Well, these did, Jamie thought. A man-servant

greeted them in a plain tiled foyer, but then opened the door into a room that made the senses swim. It was lined with books in dark wood cases, carpeted thickly underfoot, and what little of the walls was not covered with books was adorned with small tapestries and framed tiles that he thought might be Moorish. But above all, the scent! He breathed it in to the bottom of his lungs, feeling slightly intoxicated, and looking for the source of it, finally spotted the owner of this earthly paradise, sitting behind a desk and staring . . . at him. Or maybe him and Ian both; the man's eyes flicked back and forth between them, round as sucked toffees.

He straightened up instinctively, and bowed.

'We greet thee, Lord,' he said, in carefully rehearsed Hebrew. 'Peace be on your house.' The man's mouth fell open. Noticeably so; he had a large, bushy dark beard, going white near the mouth. An indefinable expression – surely it wasn't amusement? – ran over what could be seen of his face.

A small sound that certainly *was* amusement drew his attention to one side. A small brass bowl sat on a round, tile-topped table, with smoke wandering lazily up from it through a bar of late afternoon sun. Between the sun and the smoke, he could just make out the form of a woman, standing in the shadows. She stepped forward, materializing out of the gloom, and his heart jumped.

She inclined her head gravely to the soldiers, addressing them impartially.

'I am Rebekah bat-Leah Hauberger. My grand-father bids me make you welcome to our home, gentlemen,' she said, in perfect French, though the old gentleman hadn't spoken. Jamie drew in a great breath of relief; he wouldn't have to try to explain their business in Hebrew, after all. The breath was so deep, though, that it made him cough, the perfumed smoke tickling his chest.

He could feel his face going red as he tried to strangle the cough, and Ian glancing at him out of the sides of his eyes. The girl – yes, she was young, maybe his own age – swiftly took up a cover and clapped it on the bowl, then rang a bell and told the servant something in what sounded like Spanish. *Ladino?* He thought.

'Do please sit, sirs,' she said, waving gracefully toward a chair in front of the desk, then turning to fetch another standing by the wall.

'Allow me, mademoiselle!' Ian leapt forward to assist her. Jamie, still choking as quietly as possible, followed suit.

She had dark hair, very wavy, bound back from her brow with a rose-colored ribbon, but falling loose down her back, nearly to her waist. He had actually raised a hand to stroke it before catching hold of himself. Then she turned round. Pale skin, big, dark eyes, and an oddly knowing look in those eyes when she met his own — which she did, very directly, when he set the third chair down before her.

Annalise. He swallowed, hard, and cleared his throat. A wave of dizzy heat washed over him, and he wished suddenly that they'd open a window.

D'Eglise, too, was visibly relieved at having a more reliable interpreter than Jamie, and launched into a gallant speech of introduction, much decorated with French flowers, bowing repeatedly to the girl and her grandfather in turn.

Jamie wasn't paying attention to the talk; he was still watching Rebekah. It was her passing resemblance to Annalise de Marillac, the girl he'd loved in Paris, that had drawn his attention — but now he came to look, she was quite different.

Quite different. Annalise had been tiny and fluffy as a kitten. This girl was small — he'd seen that she came no higher than his elbow; her soft hair had brushed his wrist when she sat down — but there was nothing either fluffy or helpless about her. She'd noticed him watching her, and was now watching *him*, with a faint curve to her red mouth that made the blood rise in his cheeks. He coughed and looked down.

'What's amiss?' Ian muttered out of the side of his mouth. 'Ye look like ye've got a cockle-bur stuck betwixt your hurdies.'

Jamie gave an irritable twitch, then stiffened as he felt one of the rawer wounds on his back break open. He could feel the fast-cooling spot, the slow seep of pus or blood, and sat very straight, trying not to breathe deep, in hopes that the bandages would absorb the liquid before it got onto his shirt.

This niggling concern had at least distracted his mind from Rebekah bat-Leah Hauberger and to distract himself from the aggravation of his back, he returned to the three-way conversation between D'Eglise and the Jews.

The captain was sweating freely, whether from the hot tea or the strain of persuasion, but he talked easily, gesturing now and then toward his matched pair of tall, Hebrew-speaking Scots, now and then toward the window and the outer world, where vast legions of similar warriors awaited, ready and eager to do Doctor Hasdi's bidding.

The doctor watched D'Eglise intently, occasionally addressing a soft rumble of incomprehensible words to his granddaughter. It did sound like the Ladino Juanito spoke, more than anything else; certainly it sounded nothing like the Hebrew Jamie had been taught in Paris.

Finally the old Jew glanced among the three mercenaries, pursed his lips thoughtfully, and nodded. He rose and went to a large blanket-chest that stood under the window, where he knelt and carefully gathered up a long, heavy cylinder wrapped in oiled cloth. Jamie could see that it was remarkably heavy for its size, from the slow way the old man rose with it and his first thought was that it must be a gold statue of some sort. His second thought was that Rebekah smelled like rose-petals and vanilla-pods. He breathed in, very gently, feeling the shirt stick to his back.

The thing, whatever it was, jingled and chimed softly as it moved. Some sort of Jewish clock? Dr Hasdi carried the cylinder to the desk and set it down, then curled a finger to invite the soldiers to step near.

Unwrapped with a slow and solemn sense of ceremony, the object emerged from its layers of linen, canvas and oil-cloth. It *was* gold, in part, and not unlike statuary, but made of wood and shaped like a prism, with a sort of crown at one end. While Jamie was still wondering what the devil it might be, the Doctor's arthritic fingers touched a small clasp and the box opened, revealing yet more layers of cloth, from which yet another delicate, spicy scent emerged. All three soldiers breathed deep, in unison, and Rebekah made that small sound of amusement again.

'The case is cedar-wood,' she said. 'From Lebanon.'

'Oh,' D'Eglise said respectfully. 'Of course!'

The bundle inside was dressed — there was no other word for it; it was wearing a sort of caped mantle and a belt — with a miniature buckle — in velvet and embroidered silk. From one end, two massive golden finials protruded like twin heads. They were pierced work, and looked like towers, adorned in the windows and along their lower edges with a number of tiny bells.

'This is a *very* old Torah scroll,' Rebekah said, keeping a respectful distance. 'From Spain.'

'A priceless object, to be sure,' D'Eglise said, bending to peer closer.

Doctor Hasdi grunted and said something to Rebekah, who translated:

'Only to those whose Book it is. To anyone else, it has a very obvious and attractive price. If this were not so, I would not stand in need of your services.' The Doctor looked pointedly at Jamie and Ian. 'A respectable man — a Jew — will carry the Torah. It may not be touched. But you will safeguard it — and my grand-daughter.'

'Quite so, your honor.' D'Eglise flushed slightly, but was too pleased to look abashed. 'I am deeply honored by your trust, sir, and I assure you . . .' But Rebekah had rung her bell again, and the manservant came in with wine.

The job offered was simple; Rebekah was to be married to the son of the chief rabbi of the Paris synagogue. The ancient Torah was part of her dowry, as was a sum of money that made D'Eglise's eyes glisten.

The Doctor wished to engage D'Eglise to deliver all three items — the girl, the scroll, and the money — safely to Paris; the Doctor himself would travel there for the wedding, but later in the month, as his business in Bordeaux detained him. The only things to be decided were the price for D'Eglise's services, the time in which they were to be accomplished, and the guarantees D'Eglise was prepared to offer.

The Doctor's lips pursed over this last; his friend Ackerman, who had referred D'Eglise to him, had not been entirely pleased at having one of his valuable rugs stolen en route, and the Doctor wished to be assured that none of *his* valuable property — Jamie saw Rebekah's soft mouth twitch as she translated this — would go missing between Bordeaux and Paris. The Captain gave Ian and Jamie a stern look, then altered this to earnest sincerity as he assured the Doctor that there would be no difficulty; his best men would take on the job, and he would offer whatever assurances the Doctor required. Small drops of sweat stood out on his upper lip.

Between the warmth of the fire and the hot tea, Jamie was sweating, too, and could have used a glass of wine. But the old gentleman stood up abruptly, and with a courteous bow to D'Eglise, came out from behind his desk and took Jamie by the arm, pulling him up and tugging him gently toward a doorway.

He ducked, just in time to avoid braining himself on a low archway, and found himself in a small, plain room, with bunches of drying herbs hung from its beams. What —

But before he could formulate any sort of question, the old man had got hold of his shirt and was pulling it free of his plaid. He tried to step back, but there was no room, and willy-nilly, he found himself set down on a stool, the old man's horny fingers pulling loose the bandages. The doctor made a deep sound of disapproval, then shouted something in which the words *'agua caliente'* were clearly discernible, back through the archway.

He daren't stand up and flee — not and risk D'Eglises's new arrangement. And so he sat, burning with embarrassment, while the physician probed, prodded, and — a bowl of hot water having appeared — scrubbed at his back with something painfully rough. None of this bothered Jamie nearly as much as the appearance of Rebekah in the doorway, her dark eyebrows raised.

'My grandfather says your back is a mess,' she told him, translating a remark from the old man.

'Thank ye. I didna ken that,' he muttered in English, but then repeated the remark more politely in French. His cheeks burned with mortification, but a small, cold echo sounded in his heart. *'He's made a mess of you, boy.'*

The surgeon at Fort William had said it, when the soldiers had dragged Jamie to him after the flogging, legs too wabbly to stand by himself. The surgeon had been right, and so was Doctor Hasdi, but it didn't mean Jamie wanted to hear it again.

Rebekah, evidently interested to see what her grandfather meant, came round behind Jamie. He stiffened, and the doctor poked him sharply in the back of the neck, making him bend forward again. The two Jews were discussing the spectacle in tones of detachment; he felt the girl's small, soft fingers trace a line between his ribs and nearly shot off the stool, his flesh erupting in goosebumps.

'Jamie?' Ian's voice came from the hallway, sounding worried. 'Are ye all right?'

'Aye!' he managed, half-strangled. 'Don't – ye needn't come in.'

'Your name is Jamie?' Rebekah was now in front of him, leaning down to look into his face. Her own was alive with interest and concern. 'James?'

'Aye. James.' He clenched his teeth as the doctor dug a little harder, clicking his tongue.

'Diego,' she said, smiling at him. 'That's what it would be in Spanish – or Ladino. And your friend?'

'He's called Ian. That's –' he groped for a moment and found the English equivalent. 'John. That would be . . .'

'Juan. Diego and Juan.' She touched him gently on

the bare shoulder. 'You're friends? Brothers? I can see you come from the same place – where is that?'

'Friends. From . . . Scotland. The – the – Highlands. A place called Lallybroch.' He'd spoken unwarily, and a pang shot through him at the name, sharper than whatever the doctor was scraping his back with. He looked away; the girl's face was too close; he didn't want her to see.

She didn't move away. Instead, she crouched gracefully beside him and took his hand. Hers was very warm, and the hairs on his wrist rose in response, in spite of what the Doctor was doing to his back.

'It will be done soon,' she promised. 'He's cleaning the infected parts; he says they will scab over cleanly now and stop draining.' A gruff question from the doctor. 'He asks, do you have fever at night? Bad dreams?'

Startled, he looked back at her, but her face showed only compassion. Her hand tightened on his in reassurance.

'I . . . yes. Sometimes.'

A grunt from the doctor, more words, and Rebekah let go his hand with a little pat, and went out, skirts a-rustle. He closed his eyes and tried to keep the scent of her in his mind – he couldn't keep it in his nose, as the doctor was now anointing him with something vile-smelling. He could smell himself, too, and his jaw prickled with embarrassment; he reeked of stale sweat, campfire smoke, and fresh blood.

He could hear D'Eglise and Ian talking in the parlor, low-voiced, discussing whether to come and rescue him. He would have called out to them, save that he couldn't bear the captain to see . . . He pressed his lips together tight. Aye, well, it was nearly done; he could tell from the doctor's slower movements, almost gentle now.

'Rebekah!' the doctor called, impatient, and the girl appeared an instant later, a small cloth bundle in one hand. The doctor let off a short burst of words, then pressed a thin cloth of some sort over Jamie's back; it stuck to the nasty ointment.

'Grandfather says the cloth will protect your shirt until the ointment is absorbed,' she told him. 'By the time it falls off – don't peel it off, let it come off by itself – the wounds will be scabbed, but the scabs should be soft and not crack.'

The doctor took his hand off Jamie's shoulder, and Jamie shot to his feet, looking round for his shirt. Rebekah handed it to him. Her eyes were fastened on his naked chest, and he was – for the first time in his life – embarrassed by the fact that he possessed nipples. An extraordinary but not unpleasant tingle made the curly hairs on his body stand up.

'Thank you – ah, I mean . . . *gracias, Senor.*' His face was flaming, but he bowed to the doctor with as much grace as he could muster. '*Muchas gracias.*'

'*De nada,*' the old man said gruffly, with a dismissive wave of one hand. He pointed at the small bundle in his granddaughter's hand. 'Drink. No fever. No dream.' And then, surprisingly, he smiled.

'*Shalom*,' he said, and made a shooing gesture.

D'Eglise, looking pleased with the new job, left Ian and Jamie at a large tavern called *Le Poulet Gai*, where some of the other mercenaries were enjoying themselves – in various ways. The Cheerful Chicken most assuredly did boast a brothel on the upper floor, and slatternly women in various degrees of undress wandered freely through the lower rooms, picking up new customers with whom they vanished upstairs.

The two tall young Scots provoked a certain amount of interest from the women, but when Ian solemnly turned his empty purse inside out in front of them – he having put his money inside his shirt for safety – they left the lads alone.

'Couldna look at one of those,' Ian said, turning his back on the whores and devoting himself to his ale. 'Not after seein' the wee Jewess up close. Did ye ever seen anything like?'

Jamie shook his head, deep in his own drink. It was sour and fresh and went down a treat, parched as he was from the ordeal in Doctor Hasdi's surgery. He could still smell the ghost of Rebekah's scent, vanilla and roses, a fugitive fragrance among the reeks of the tavern. He fumbled in his sporran, bringing out the little cloth bundle Rebekah had given him.

'She said — well, the Doctor said — I was to drink this. How, d'ye think?' The bundle held a mixture of broken leaves, small sticks, and a coarse powder, and smelled strongly of something he'd never smelled before. Not bad; just odd. Ian frowned at it.

'Well . . . ye'd brew a tea of it, I suppose,' he said. 'How else?'

'I havena got anything to brew it in,' Jamie said. 'I was thinkin' . . . maybe put it in the ale?'

'Why not?'

Ian wasn't paying much attention; he was watching Mathieu Pig-face, who was standing against a wall, summoning whores as they passed by, looking them up and down, and occasionally fingering the merchandise before sending each one on with a smack on the rear.

He wasn't really tempted — the women scairt him, to be honest — but he was curious. If he ever *should* . . . how did ye start? Just grab, like Mathieu was doing, or did ye need to ask about the price first, to be sure you could afford it? And was it proper to bargain, like ye did for a loaf of bread or a flitch of bacon, or would the woman kick ye in the privates and find someone less mean?

He shot a glance at Jamie, who, after a bit of choking, had got his herbed ale down all right and was looking a little glazed. He didn't think Jamie knew, either, but he didn't want to ask, just in case he did.

'I'm goin' to the privy,' Jamie said abruptly and stood up. He looked pale.

'Have ye got the shits?'

'Not yet.' With this ominous remark, he was off, bumping into tables in his haste, and Ian followed, pausing long enough to thriftily drain the last of Jamie's ale as well as his own.

Mathieu had found one he liked; he leered at Ian and said something obnoxious as he ushered his choice toward the stairs. Ian smiled cordially and said something much worse in *Gaidhlig*.

By the time he got to the yard at the back of the tavern, Jamie had disappeared. Figuring he'd be back as soon as he rid himself of his trouble, Ian leaned tranquilly against the back wall of the building, enjoying the cool night air and watching the folk in the yard.

There were a couple of torches burning, stuck in the ground, and it looked a bit like a painting he'd seen of the Last Judgement, with angels on the one side blowing trumpets and sinners on the other, going down to Hell in a tangle of naked limbs and bad behavior. It was mostly sinners out here, though now and then he thought he saw an angel floating past the corner of his eye. He licked his lips thoughtfully, wondering what was in the stuff Doctor Hasdi had given Jamie.

Jamie himself emerged from the privy at the far side of the yard, looking a little more settled in himself, and spotting Ian, made his way through the little knots of drinkers sitting on the ground singing, and the others wandering to and fro, smiling vaguely as they looked for something, not knowing what they were looking for.

Ian was seized by a sudden sense of revulsion, almost terror; a fear that he would never see Scotland again, would die here, among strangers.

'We should go home,' he said abruptly, as soon as Jamie was in earshot. 'As soon as we've finished this job.'

'Home?' Jamie looked strangely at Ian, as though he were speaking some incomprehensible language.

'Ye've business there, and so have I. We —'

A skelloch and the thud and clatter of a falling table with its burden of dishes interrupted them. The back door of the tavern burst open and a woman ran out, yelling in a sort of French that Ian didn't understand but knew fine was bad words from the tone of it. Similar words in a loud male voice, and big Mathieu charged out after her.

He caught her by the shoulder, spun her round and cracked her across the face with the back of one meaty hand. Ian flinched at the sound, and Jamie's hand tightened on his wrist.

'What –' Jamie began, but then stopped dead.

'*Putain de* . . . *merde* . . . *tu fais* . . . *chier*,' Mathieu panted, slapping her with each word. She shrieked some more, trying to get away, but he had her by the arm, and now jerked her round and pushed her hard in the back, knocking her to her knees.

Jamie's hand loosened, and Ian grabbed his arm, tight.

'Don't,' he said tersely, and yanked Jamie back into the shadow.

'I wasn't,' Jamie said, but under his breath and not noticing much what he was saying, because his eyes were fixed on what was happening, as much as Ian's were.

The light from the door spilled over the woman, glowing off her hanging breasts, bared in the ripped neck of her shift. Glowing off her wide round buttocks, too; Mathieu had shoved her skirts up to her waist and was behind her, jerking at his flies one-handed, the other hand twisted in her hair so her head pulled back, throat straining and her face white-eyed as a panicked horse.

'Pute!' he said, and gave her arse a loud smack, open-handed. 'Nobody says no to me!' He'd got his cock out now, in his hand, and shoved it into the woman with a violence that made her hurdies wobble and knotted Ian from knees to neck.

'Merde,' Jamie said, still under his breath. Other men and a couple of women had come out into the yard and were gathered round with the others, enjoying the spectacle as Mathieu set to work in a business-like manner. He let go of the woman's hair in order to grasp her by the hips and her head hung down, hair hiding her face. She grunted with each thrust, panting bad words that made the onlookers laugh.

Ian was shocked – and shocked as much at his own arousal as at what Mathieu was doing. He'd not seen open coupling before, only the heaving and giggling of things happening under a blanket, now and then a wee flash of pale flesh. This . . . He ought to look away, he knew that fine. But he didn't.

Jamie took in a breath, but no telling whether he meant to say something. Mathieu threw back his big head and howled like a wolf and the watchers all cheered. Then his face convulsed, gapped teeth showing in a grin like a skull's, and he made a noise like a pig gives out when you knock it clean on the head, and collapsed on top of the whore.

The whore squirmed out from under his bulk,

abusing him roundly. Ian understood what she was saying now, and would have been shocked anew, if he'd had any capacity for being shocked left. She hopped up, evidently not hurt, and kicked Mathieu in the ribs once, then twice, but having no shoes on, didn't hurt him. She reached for the purse still tied at his waist, stuck her hand in and grabbed a handful of coins, then kicked him once more for luck and stomped off into the house, holding up the neck of her shift. Mathieu lay sprawled on the ground, his breeks around his thighs, laughing and wheezing.

Ian heard Jamie swallow, and realized he was still gripping Jamie's arm. Jamie didn't seem to have noticed. Ian let go. His face was burning all the way down to the middle of his chest, and he didn't think it was just torchlight on Jamie's face, either.

'Let's . . . go someplace else,' he said.

'I wish we'd . . . done something,' Jamie blurted. They hadn't spoken at all after leaving the *Poulet Gai.* They'd walked clear to the other end of the street and down a side alley, eventually coming to rest in a small tavern, fairly quiet. Juanito and Raoul were there, dicing with some locals, but gave Ian and Jamie no more than a glance.

'I dinna see what we *could* have done,' Ian said

reasonably. 'I mean, we could maybe have taken on Mathieu together and got off with only bein' maimed. But ye ken it would ha' started a kebbie-lebbie, wi' all the others there.' He hesitated, and gave Jamie a quick glance before returning his gaze to his cup. 'And . . . she *was* a whore. I mean, she wasna a —'

'I ken what ye mean.' Jamie cut him off. 'Aye, ye're right. And she did go with the man, to start. God knows what he did to make her take against him, but there's likely plenty to choose from. I wish — ah, feckit. D'ye want something to eat?'

Ian shook his head. The barmaid brought them a jug of wine, glanced at them and dismissed them as negligible. It was rough wine that took the skin off the insides of your mouth, but it had a decent taste to it, under the resin fumes, and wasn't too much watered. Jamie drank deep, and faster than he generally did; he was uneasy in his skin, prickling and irritable, and wanted the feeling to go away.

There were a few women in the place, not many. Jamie had to think that whoring maybe wasn't a profitable business, wretched as most of the poor creatures looked, raddled and half-toothless. Maybe it wore them down, having to . . . He turned away from the thought and finding the jug empty, waved to the barmaid for another.

Juanito gave a joyful whoop and said something in Ladino. Looking in that direction, Jamie saw one of the whores who'd been lurking in the shadows come gliding purposefully in, bending down to give Juanito a congratulatory kiss as he scooped in his winnings. Jamie snorted a little, trying to blow the smell of her out of his neb — she'd passed by close enough that he'd got a good whiff of her; a stink of rancid sweat and dead fish. Alexandre had told him that was from unclean privates, and he believed it.

He went back to the wine. Ian was matching him, cup for cup, and likely for the same reason. His friend wasn't usually irritable or crankit, but if he was well put out, he'd often stay that way until the next dawn — a good sleep erased his bad temper, but 'til then you didn't want to rile him.

He shot a sidelong glance at Ian. He couldn't tell Ian about Jenny. He just . . . couldn't. But neither could he think about her, left alone at Lallybroch . . . maybe with ch —

'Oh, God,' he said, under his breath. 'No. Please. No.'

'*Dinna come back*,' Murtagh had said, and plainly meant it. Well, he *would* go back — but not yet awhile. It wouldn't help his sister, him going back just now and bringing Randall and the redcoats straight to her like flies to a fresh-killed deer . . . He shoved that analogy hastily out of sight, horrified. The truth was, it made him sick with shame to think about

Jenny, and he tried not to – and was the more ashamed because he mostly succeeded.

Ian's gaze was fixed on another of the harlots. She was old, in her thirties at least, but had most of her teeth and was cleaner than most. She was flirting with Juanito and Raoul, too, and Jamie wondered whether she'd mind if she found out they were Jews. Maybe a whore couldn't afford to be choosy.

His treacherous mind at once presented him with a picture of his sister, obliged to follow that walk of life to feed herself, made to take any man who . . . Blessed Mother, what would the folk, the tenants, the servants, do to her if they found out what had happened? The talk . . . He shut his eyes tight, hoping to block the vision.

'That one's none sae bad,' Ian said meditatively, and Jamie opened his eyes. The better-looking whore had bent over Juanito, deliberately rubbing her breast against his warty ear. 'If she doesna mislike a Jew, maybe she'd . . .'

The blood flamed up in Jamie's face.

'If ye've got any thought to my sister, ye're no going to – to – pollute yourself wi' a French whore!'

Ian's face went blank, but then flooded with color in turn.

'Oh, aye? And if I said your sister wasna worth it?'

Jamie's fist caught him in the eye and he flew backward, overturning the bench and crashing into the next table. Jamie scarcely noticed, the agony in his hand shooting fire and brimstone from his crushed knuckles up his forearm. He rocked to and fro, injured hand clutched between his thighs, cursing freely in three languages.

Ian sat on the floor, bent over, holding his eye and breathing through his mouth in short gasps. After a minute, he straightened up. His eye was puffing already, leaking tears down his lean cheek. He got up, shaking his head slowly, and put the bench back in place. Then he sat down, picked up his cup and took a deep gulp, put it down and blew out his breath. He took the snot-rag Jamie was holding out to him and dabbed at his eye.

'Sorry,' Jamie managed. The agony in his hand was beginning to subside, but the anguish in his heart wasn't.

'Aye,' Ian said quietly, not meeting his eye. 'I wish we'd done something, too. Ye want to share a bowl o' stew?'

Two days later, they set off for Paris. After some thought, D'Eglise had decided that Rebekah and her maid would travel by coach, escorted by Jamie and Ian. D'Eglise and the rest of the troop would take the money, with some men sent ahead in small groups to wait, both to check the road ahead, and so that they could ride in shifts, not stopping anywhere along the way. The women obviously would have to stop, but if they had nothing valuable with them, they'd be in no danger.

It was only when they went to collect the women at Doctor Hasdi's residence that they learned the Torah scroll and its custodian, a sober-looking man of middle-age introduced to them as Monsieur Peretz, would be traveling with Rebekah. 'I trust my greatest treasures to you, gentlemen,' the Doctor told them, through his grand-daughter, and gave them a formal little bow.

'May you find us worthy of trust, Lord,' Jamie managed in halting Hebrew, and Ian bowed with great solemnity, hand on his heart. Doctor Hasdi looked from one to the other, gave a small nod, and then stepped forward to kiss Rebekah on the forehead.

'Go with God, child,' he whispered, in something close enough to Spanish that Jamie understood it.

All went well for the first day, and the first night. The autumn weather held fine, with no more than a pleasant tang of chill in the air, and the horses were sound. Doctor Hasdi had provided Jamie with a purse to cover the expenses of the journey, and they all ate decently and slept at a very respectable inn – Ian being sent in first to inspect the premises and insure against any nasty surprises.

The next day dawned cloudy, but the wind came up and blew the clouds away before noon, leaving the sky clean and brilliant as a sapphire overhead. Jamie was riding in the van, Ian post, and the coach was making good time, in spite of a rutted, winding road.

As they reached the top of a small rise, though, Jamie brought his horse to a sudden stop, raising a hand to halt the coach, and Ian reined up alongside him. A small stream had run through the roadbed in the dip below, making a bog some ten feet across.

'What –' he began, but was interrupted. The driver had pulled his team up for an instant, but at a peremptory shout from inside the coach, now snapped the reins over the horses' backs and the coach lunged forward, narrowly missing Jamie's horse, which shied violently, flinging its rider off into the bushes.

'Jamie! Are ye all right?' Torn between concern for his friend and for his duty, Ian held his horse, glancing to and fro.

'Stop them! Get them! *Ifrinn!*' Jamie scuttled crabwise out of the weeds, face scratched and bright red with fury. Ian didn't wait, but kicked his horse and lit out in pursuit of the heavy coach, this now lurching from side to side as it ran down into the boggy bottom. Shrill feminine cries of protest from inside were drowned by the driver's exclamation of *'Ladrones!'*

That was one word he kent in Spanish – 'thieves'. One of the *ladrones* was already skittering up the side of the coach like an eight-legged cob, and the driver promptly dived off the box, hit the ground and ran for it.

'Coward!' Ian bellowed, and gave out with a Hieland screech that set the coach-horses dancing, flinging their heads to and fro, and giving the would-be kidnapper fits with the reins. He forced his own horse – who hadn't liked the screeching any better than the coach-horses – through the narrow gap between the brush and the coach, and as he came even with the driver, had his pistol out. He drew down on the fellow – a young chap with long yellow hair – and shouted at him to pull up.

The man glanced at him, crouched low and slapped the reins on the horses' backs, shouting at them in a voice like iron. Ian fired, and missed – but the delay had let Jamie catch them up; he saw Jamie's red head poke up as he climbed the back of the coach, and there were more screams from inside as Jamie pounded across the roof and launched himself at the yellow-haired driver.

Leaving that bit of trouble to Jamie to deal with, Ian kicked his horse forward, meaning to get ahead and seize the reins, but another of the thieves had beat him to it and was hauling down on one horse's head. Aye, well, it worked once. Ian inflated his lungs as far as they'd go and let rip.

The coach-horses bolted in a spray of mud. Jamie and the yellow-haired driver fell off the box, and the whoreson in the road disappeared, possibly trampled into the mire. Ian hoped so. Blood in his eye, he reined up his own agitated mount, drew his broadsword and charged across the road, shrieking like a *ban-sidhe* and slashing wildly. Two thieves stared up at him open-mouthed, then broke and ran for it.

He chased them a wee bit into the brush, but the going was too thick for his horse, and he turned back to find Jamie rolling about in the road, earnestly hammering the yellow-haired laddie. Ian hesitated — help him, or see to the coach? A loud crash and horrible screams decided him at once and he charged down the road.

The coach, driver-less, had run off the road, hit the bog and fallen sideways into a ditch. From the clishmaclaver coming from inside, he thought the women were likely all right, and swinging off his horse, wrapped the reins hastily round a tree and went to take care of the coach-horses before they killed themselves.

It took no little while to disentangle the mess single-handed — luckily the horses had not managed to damage themselves significantly – and his efforts were not aided by the emergence from the coach of two agitated and very disheveled women carrying on in an incomprehensible mix of French and Ladino.

Just as well, he thought, giving them a vague wave of a hand he could ill-spare at the moment. *It wouldna help to hear what they're saying.* Then he picked up the word 'dead,' and changed his mind. Monsieur Peretz was normally so silent that Ian had in fact forgotten his presence, in the confusion of the moment. He was even more silent now, Ian learned, having broken his neck when the coach overturned.

'Oh, Jesus,' he said, running to look. But the man was undeniably dead, and the horses were still creating a ruckus, slipping and stamping in the mud of the ditch. He was too busy for a bit to worry about how Jamie was faring, but as he got the second horse detached from the coach and safely tethered to a tree, he did begin to wonder where the wean was.

He didn't think it safe to leave the women; the banditti might come back, and a right numpty he'd look if they did. There was no sign of their driver, who had evidently abandoned them out of fright. He told the ladies to sit down under a sycamore tree and gave them his canteen to drink from, and after a bit, they stopped talking quite so fast.

'Where is Diego?' Rebekah said, quite intelligibly.

'Och, he'll be along presently,' Ian said, hoping it was true. He was beginning to be worrit, himself.

'Perhaps he's been killed, too,' said the maid-servant, who shot an ill-tempered glare at her mistress. 'How would you feel then?'

'I'm sure he wouldn't – I mean, he's not. I'm sure,' Rebekah repeated, not sounding all that sure.

She was right, though; no sooner had Ian decided to march the women back along the road to have a keek, when Jamie came shambling around the bend himself, and sank down in the dry grass, closing his eyes.

'Are you all right?' Rebekah asked, bending down anxiously to look at him from under the brim of her straw traveling hat. He didn't look very peart, Ian thought.

'Aye, fine.' He touched the back of his head, wincing slightly. 'Just a wee dunt on the heid. The fellow who fell down in the road,' he explained to Ian, closing his eyes again. 'He got up again, and hit me from behind. Didna knock me clean out, but it distracted me for a wee bit, and when I got my wits back, they'd both gone – the fellow that hit me, and the one I was hittin'.'

'Mmphm,' said Ian, and squatting in front of his friend, thumbed up one of Jamie's eyelids and peered intently into the bloodshot blue eye behind it. He had no idea what to look for, but he'd seen *Pere* Renault do that, after which he usually applied leeches somewhere. As it was, both that eye and the other one looked fine to him; just as well, as he hadn't any leeches. He handed Jamie the canteen and went to look the horses over.

'Two of them are sound enough,' he reported, coming back. 'The light bay's lame. Did the bandits take your horse? And what about the driver?'

Jamie looked surprised.

'I forgot I had a horse,' he confessed. 'I dinna ken about the driver – didna see him lyin' in the road, at least.' He glanced vaguely round. 'Where's Monsiuer Pickle?'

'Dead. Stay there, aye?'

Ian sighed, got up and loped back down the road, where he found no sign of the driver, though he walked to and fro calling for a while. Fortunately he did find Jamie's horse, peaceably cropping grass by the verge. He rode it back, and found the women on their feet, discussing something in low voices, now and then looking down the road, or standing on their toes in a vain attempt to see through the trees.

Jamie was still sitting on the ground, eyes closed – but at least upright.

'Can ye ride, man?' Ian asked softly, squatting down by his friend. To his relief, Jamie opened his eyes at once.

'Oh, aye. Ye're thinkin' we should ride into

Saint-Aubaye, and send someone back to do something about the coach and Peretz?'

'What else is there to do?'

'Nothing I can think of. I dinna suppose we can take him with us.' Jamie got to his feet, swaying a little, but without needing to hold onto the tree. 'Can the women ride, d'ye think?'

Marie could, it turned out – at least a little. Rebekah had never been on a horse. After more discussion than Ian would have believed possible on the subject, he got the late M. Peretz decently laid out on the coach's seat with a handkerchief over his face against flies, and the rest of them finally mounted: Jamie on his horse with the Torah scroll in its canvas wrappings bound behind his saddle – between the profanation of its being touched by a Gentile and the prospect of its being left in the coach for anyone happening by to find, the women had reluctantly allowed the former – the maid on one of the coach horses, with a makeshift pair of saddlebags made from the covers of the coach's seats, these filled with as much of the women's luggage as they could cram into them, and Ian with Rebekah on the saddle before him.

Rebekah looked like a wee dolly, but she was surprisingly solid, as he found when she put her foot in his hands and he tossed her up into the saddle. She didn't manage to swing her leg over, and instead lay across the saddle like a dead deer, waving her arms and legs in agitation. Wrestling her into an upright position, and getting himself set behind her, left him red-faced and sweating, far more than dealing with the horses had.

Jamie gave him a raised eyebrow, as much jealousy as amusement in it, and he gave Jamie a squinted eye in return and put his arm round Rebekah's waist to settle her against him, hoping that he didn't stink too badly.

It was dark by the time they made it into Saint-Aubaye and found an inn that could provide them with two rooms. Ian talked to the landlord, and arranged that someone should go in the morning to retrieve M. Peretz's body and bury it; the women weren't happy about the lack of proper preparation of the body, but as they insisted he must be buried before the next sundown, there wasn't much else to be done. Then he inspected the women's room, looked under the beds, rattled the shutters in a confident manner, and bade them goodnight. They looked that wee bit frazzled.

Going back to the other room, he heard a sweet chiming sound, and found Jamie on his knees, pushing the bundle that contained the Torah scroll under the single bed.

'That'll do,' he said, sitting back on his heels with a sigh. He looked nearly as done-in as the women, Ian thought, but didn't say so.

'I'll go and have some supper sent up,' he said. 'I smelled a joint roasting. Some of that, and maybe –'

'Whatever they've got,' Jamie said fervently. 'Bring it all.'

They ate heartily, and separately, in their rooms. Jamie was beginning to feel that the second helping of *tarte tatin* with clotted cream had been a mistake, when Rebekah came into the men's room, followed by her maid carrying a small tray with a jug on it, wisping aromatic steam. Jamie sat up straight, restraining a small cry as pain flashed through his head. Rebekah frowned at him, gull-winged brows lowering in concern.

'Your head hurts very much, Diego?'

'No, it's fine. No but a weè bang on the heid.' He was sweating and his wame was wobbly, but he pressed his hands flat on the wee table and was sure he looked steady. She appeared not to think so, and came close, bending down to look searchingly into his eyes.

'I don't think so,' she said. 'You look . . . clammy.'

'Oh. Aye?' he said, rather feebly.

'If she means ye look like a fresh-shucked clam,

then aye, ye do,' Ian informed him. 'Shocked, ken? All pale and wet and —'

'I ken what clammy means, aye?' He glowered at Ian, who gave him half a grin — damn, he must look awful; Ian was actually worried. He swallowed, looking for something witty to say in reassurance, but his gorge rose suddenly and he was obliged to shut both mouth and eyes tightly, concentrating fiercely to make it go back down.

'Tea,' Rebekah was saying firmly. She took the jug from her maid and poured a cup, then folded Jamie's hands about it, and holding his hands with her own, guided the cup to his mouth. 'Drink. It will help.'

He drank, and it did. At least he felt less queasy at once. He recognized the taste of the tea, though he thought this cup had a few other things in it, too.

'Again.' Another cup was presented; he managed to drink this one alone, and by the time it was down, felt a good bit better. His head still throbbed with his heartbeat, but the pain seemed be standing a little apart from him, somehow.

'You shouldn't be left alone for a little while,' Rebekah informed him, and sat down, sweeping her skirts elegantly around her ankles. He opened his mouth to say that he wasn't alone, Ian was there — but caught Ian's eye in time and stopped.

'The bandits,' she was saying to Ian, her pretty brow creased, 'who do you think that they were?'

'Ah . . . well, depends. If they kent who ye were, and wanted to abduct ye, that's one thing. But could be they were no but random thieves, and saw the coach and thought they'd chance it for what they might get. Ye didna recognize any of them, did ye?'

Her eyes sprang wide. They weren't quite the color of Annalise's, Jamie thought hazily. A softer brown . . . like the breast feathers on a grouse.

'Know who I was?' she whispered. 'Wanted to abduct me?' She swallowed. 'You . . . think that's possible?' She gave a little shudder.

'Well, I dinna ken, of course. Here, *a nighean*, ye ought to have a wee nip of that tea, I'm thinkin'.' Ian stretched out a long arm for the jug, but she moved it back, shaking her head.

'No, it's medicine — and Diego needs it. Don't you?' she said, leaning a little forward to peer earnestly into Jamie's eyes. She'd taken off the hat, but had her hair tucked up — mostly — in a lacy white cap with pink ribbon. He nodded obediently.

'Marie — bring some brandy, please. The shock . . .' She swallowed again, and wrapped her arms briefly around herself. Jamie noticed the way it pushed her breasts up, so they swelled just a little above her stays. There was a little tea left in his cup; he drank it automatically.

Marie came with the brandy, and poured a glass for Rebekah — then one for Ian, at Rebekah's gesture, and when Jamie made a small polite noise in his throat, half-filled his cup, pouring in more tea on top of it. The taste was peculiar, but he didn't really mind. The pain had gone off to the far side of the room; he could see it sitting over there, a wee glowering sort of purple thing with a bad-tempered expression on its face. He laughed at it, and Ian frowned at him.

'What are ye giggling at?'

Jamie couldn't think how to describe the pain-beastie, so just shook his head, which proved a mistake — the pain looked suddenly gleeful and shot back into his head with a noise like tearing cloth. The room spun and he clutched the table with both hands.

'Diego!' Chairs scraped and there was a good bit of clishmaclaver that he paid no attention to. Next thing he knew, he was lying on the bed looking at the ceiling beams. One of them seemed to be twining slowly, like a vine growing.

'. . . and he told the captain that there was someone among the Jews who kent about . . .' Ian's voice was soothing, earnest and slow so Rebekah would understand him — though Jamie thought she maybe understood more than she said. The twining beam was slowly sprouting small green leaves, and he had the faint thought that this was unusual, but a great sense of tranquility had come over him and he didn't mind it a bit.

Rebekah was saying something now, her voice

soft and worried, and with some effort, he turned his head to look. She was leaning over the table toward Ian, and he had both big hands wrapped round hers, reassuring her that he and Jamie would let no harm come to her.

A different face came suddenly into his view; the maid, Marie, frowning down at him. She rudely pulled back his eyelid and peered into his eye, so close he could smell the garlic on her breath. He blinked hard, and she let go with a small 'hmph!', then turned to say something to Rebekah, who replied in quick Ladino. The maid shook her head dubiously, but left the room.

Her face didn't leave with her, though. He could still see it, frowning down at him from above. It had become attached to the leafy beam, and he now realized that there was a snake up there, a serpent with a woman's head, and an apple in its mouth – that couldn't be right, surely it should be a pig? – and it came slithering down the wall and right over his chest, pressing the apple close to his face. It smelled wonderful, and he wanted to bite it, but before he could, he felt the weight of the snake change, going soft and heavy, and he arched his back a little, feeling the distinct imprint of big round breasts squashing against him. The snake's tail – she was mostly a woman now, but her backend seemed still to be snakeish – was delicately stroking the inside of his thigh.

He made a very high-pitched noise, and Ian came hurriedly to the bed.

'Are ye all right, man?'

'I – oh. Oh! Oh, Jesus, do that again.'

'Do *what* –' Ian was beginning, when Rebekah appeared, putting a hand on Ian's arm.

'Don't worry,' she said, looking intently at Jamie. 'He's all right. The medicine – it gives men strange dreams.'

'He doesna look like he's asleep,' Ian said dubiously. In fact, Jamie was squirming – or thought he was squirming – on the bed, trying to persuade the lower half of the snake-woman to change, too. He *was* panting; he could hear himself.

'It's a waking dream,' Rebekah said reassuringly. 'Come, leave him. He'll fall quite asleep in a bit, you'll see.'

Jamie didn't think he'd fallen asleep, but it was evidently some time later that he emerged from a remarkable tryst with the snake-demon – he didn't know how he knew she was a demon, but clearly she was – who had not changed her lower half, but had a very womanly mouth about her – and a number of her friends, these being small female demons who licked his ears – and other things – with great enthusiasm.

He turned his head on the pillow to allow one of these better access and saw, with no sense of surprise,

Ian kissing Rebekah. The brandy bottle had fallen over, empty, and he seemed to see the wraith of its perfume rise swirling through the air like smoke, wrapping the two of them in a mist shot with rainbows.

He closed his eyes again, the better to attend to the snake-lady, who now had a number of new and interesting acquaintances. When he opened them some time later, Ian and Rebekah were gone.

At some point, he heard Ian give a sort of strangled cry and wondered dimly what had happened, but it didn't seem important, and the thought drifted away. He slept.

He woke sometime later, feeling limp as a frostbitten cabbage leaf, but the pain in his head was gone. He just lay there for a bit, enjoying the feeling. It was dark in the room, and it was some time before he realized from the smell of brandy that Ian was lying beside him.

Memory came back to him. It took a little time to disentangle the real memories from the memory of dreams, but he was quite sure he'd seen Ian embracing Rebekah — and her, him. What the devil had happened *then*?

Ian wasn't asleep; he could tell. His friend lay rigid

as one of the tomb-figures in the crypt at St Denis, and his breathing was rapid and shaky, as though he'd just run a mile uphill. Jamie cleared his throat, and Ian jerked as though stabbed with a brooch-pin.

'Aye, so?' he whispered, and Ian's breathing stopped abruptly. He swallowed, audibly.

'If ye breathe a word of this to your sister,' he said in an impassioned whisper, 'I'll stab ye in your sleep, cut off your heid, and kick it to Arles and back.'

Jamie didn't want to think about his sister, and he did want to hear about Rebekah, so he merely said, 'Aye. So?'

Ian made a small grunting noise, indicative of thinking how best to begin, and turned over in his plaid, facing Jamie.

'Aye, well. Ye raved a bit about the naked she-devils ye were havin' it away with, and I didna think the lass should have to be hearing that manner o' thing, so I said we should go into the other room, and –

'Was this before or after ye started kissing her?' Jamie asked. Ian inhaled strongly through his nose.

'After,' he said tersely. 'And she was kissin' me back, aye?'

'Aye, I noticed that. So then . . . ?' He could feel Ian squirming slowly, like a worm on a hook, but waited. It often took Ian a moment to find words, but it was usually worth waiting for. Certainly in this instance.

He was a little shocked — and frankly envious — and he did wonder what might happen when the lass's affianced discovered she wasn't a virgin, but he supposed the man might not find out; she seemed a clever lass. It might be wise to leave D'Eglise's troop, though, and head south, just in case . . .

'D'ye think it hurts a lot to be circumcised?' Ian asked suddenly.

'I do. How could it not?' His hand sought out his own member, protectively rubbing a thumb over the bit in question. True, it wasn't a very big bit, but . . .

'Well, they do it to wee bairns,' Ian pointed out. 'Canna be that bad, can it?'

'Mmphm,' Jamie said, unconvinced, though fairness made him add, 'Aye, well, and they did it to Christ, too.'

'Aye?' Ian sounded startled. 'Aye, I suppose so — I hadna thought o' that.'

'Well, ye dinna think of Him bein' a Jew, do ye? But He was, to start.'

There was a momentary, meditative silence before Ian spoke again.

'D'ye think Jesus ever did it? Wi' a lass, I mean, before he went to preachin'?'

'I think *Pere* Renault's goin' to have ye for blasphemy, next thing.'

Ian twitched, as though worried that the priest might be lurking in the shadows.

'*Pere* Renault's nowhere near here, thank God.'

'Aye, but ye'll need to confess yourself to him, won't ye?'

Ian shot upright, clutching his plaid around him. 'What?'

'Ye'll go to hell, else, if ye get killed,' Jamie pointed out, feeling rather smug. There was moonlight through the window and he could see Ian's face, drawn in anxious thought, his deepset eyes darting right and left from Scylla to Charybdis. Suddenly Ian turned his head toward Jamie, having spotted the possibility of an open channel between the threats of hell and *Pere* Renault.

'I'd only go to hell if it was a mortal sin,' he said. 'If it's no but venial, I'd only have to spend a thousand years or so in Purgatory. That wouldna be so bad.'

'Of course it's a mortal sin,' Jamie said, cross. 'Anybody kens fornication's a mortal sin, ye numpty.'

'Aye, but . . .' Ian made a 'wait a bit' gesture with one hand, deep in thought. 'To be a *mortal* sin, though, ye've got the three things. Requirements, like.' He put up an index finger. 'It's got to be seriously wrong.' Middle finger. 'Ye've got to *know* it's seriously wrong.' Ring finger. 'And ye've got to give full consent to it. That's the way of it, aye?' He put his hand down and looked at Jamie, brows raised.

'Aye, and which part of that did ye not do? The

full consent? Did she rape ye?' He was chaffing, but Ian turned his face away in a manner that gave him a sudden doubt. 'Ian?'

'Noo . . .' his friend said, but it sounded doubtful, too. 'It wasna like that – exactly. I meant more the seriously wrong part. I dinna think it was . . .' his voice trailed off.

Jamie flung himself over, raised on one elbow.

'Ian,' he said, steel in his voice. 'What did ye *do* to the lass? If ye took her maidenheid, it's seriously wrong. Especially with her betrothed. Oh – ' a thought occurred to him, and he leaned a little closer, lowering his voice. 'Was she no a virgin? Maybe that's different.' If the lass was an out and out wanton, perhaps . . . she probably *did* write poetry, come to think . . .

Ian had now folded his arms on his knees and was resting his forehead on them, his voice muffled in the folds of his plaid. '. . . dinna ken . . .' emerged in a strangled croak.

Jamie reached out and dug his fingers hard into Ian's calf, making his friend unfold with a startled cry that made someone in a distant chamber shift and grunt in their sleep.

'What d'ye mean ye dinna ken? How could ye not notice?' he hissed.

'Ah . . . well . . . she . . . erm . . . she did me wi' her hand,' Ian blurted. 'Before I could . . . well.'

'Oh.' Jamie rolled onto his back, somewhat deflated in spirit, if not in flesh. His cock seemed still to want to hear the details.

'Is that seriously wrong?' Ian asked, turning his face toward Jamie again. 'Or – well, I canna say I really gave full *consent* to it, because that wasna what I had in mind doing at all, but . . .'

'I think ye're headed for the Bad Place,' Jamie assured him. 'Ye meant to do it, whether ye managed or not. And how did it happen, come to that? Did she just . . . take hold?'

Ian let out a long, long sigh, and sank his head in his hands. He looked as though it hurt.

'Well, we kissed for a bit, and there was more brandy – lots more. She . . . er . . . she'd take a mouthful and kiss me and er . . . put it into my mouth, and . . .'

'*Ifrinn!*'

'Will ye not say "Hell!" like that, please? I dinna want to think about it.'

'Sorry. Go on. Did she let ye feel her breasts?'

'Just a bit. She wouldna take her stays off, but I could feel her nipples through her shift – did ye say something?'

'No,' Jamie said with an effort. 'What then?'

'Well, she put her hand under my kilt and then pulled it out again like she'd touched a snake.'

'And had she?'

'She had, aye. She was shocked. Will ye no snort like that?' he said, annoyed. 'Ye'll wake the whole house. It was because it wasna circumcised.'

'Oh. Is that why she wouldna . . . er . . . the regular way?'

'She didna say so, but maybe. After a bit, though, she wanted to look at it, and that's when . . . well.'

'Mmphm.' Naked demons versus the chance of damnation or not, Jamie thought Ian had had well the best of it this evening. A thought occurred to him. 'Why did ye ask if being circumcised hurts? Ye werena thinking of doing it, were ye? For her, I mean?'

'I wouldna say the thought hadna occurred to me,' Ian admitted. 'I mean . . . I thought I should maybe marry her, under the circumstances. But I suppose I couldna become a Jew, even if I got up the nerve to be circumcised – my mam would tear my heid off if I did.'

'No, ye're right,' Jamie agreed. 'She would. *And* ye'd go to Hell.' The thought of the rare and delicate Rebekah churning butter in the yard of a Highland croft or waulking urine-soaked wool with her bare feet was slightly more ludicrous than the vision of Ian in a skull-cap and whiskers – but not by much. 'Besides, ye havena got any money, have ye?'

'A bit,' Ian said thoughtfully. 'Not enough to go and live in Timbuktoo, though, and I'd have to go at least that far.'

Jamie sighed and stretched, easing himself. A meditative silence fell, Ian no doubt contemplating perdition, Jamie reliving the better bits of his opium dreams, but with Rebekah's face on the snake-lady. Finally he broke the silence, turning to his friend.

'So . . . was it worth the chance of goin' to Hell?'

Ian sighed long and deep once more, but it was the sigh of a man at peace with himself.

'Oh, aye.'

Jamie woke at dawn, feeling altogether well, and in a much better frame of mind. Some kindly soul had brought a jug of sour ale and some bread and cheese. He refreshed himself with these as he dressed, pondering the day's work.

He'd have to collect a few men to go back and deal with the coach. He supposed the best thing to do with M. Peretz was to fetch him here *in* the coach, and then see if there were any Jews in the vicinity who might be prevailed upon to bury him – the women insisted that he ought to be buried before sundown. If not . . . well, he'd cross that road when he came to it.

He thought the coach wasn't badly damaged; they might get it back upon the road again by noon . . . How far might it be to Bonnes? That was the next town with an inn. If it was too far, or the coach too badly hurt, or he couldn't dispose decently of M. Peretz, they'd need to stay the night here again. He fingered his purse, but thought he had enough for another night and the hire of men; the Doctor had been generous.

He was beginning to wonder what was keeping Ian and the women. Though he kent women took more time to do anything than a man would, let alone getting dressed – well, they had stays and the like to fret with, after all . . . He sipped ale, contemplating a vision of Rebekah's stays, and the very vivid images his mind had been conjuring ever since Ian's description of his encounter with the lass. He could all but see her nipples through the thin fabric of her shift, smooth and round as pebbles . . .

Ian burst through the door, wild-eyed, his hair standing on end.

'They're gone!'

Jamie choked on his ale.

'What? How?'

Ian understood what he meant, and was already heading for the bed.

'No one took them. There's nay sign of a struggle, and their things are gone. The window's open, and the shutters aren't broken.'

Jamie was on his knees alongside Ian, thrusting first his hands and then his head and shoulders under the bed. There was a canvas-wrapped bundle there, and he was flooded with a momentary relief – which disappeared the instant Ian dragged it into the light. It made a noise, but not the gentle chime of golden bells. It rattled, and when Jamie seized the corner of the canvas and unrolled it, the contents were shown to be nought but sticks and stones, these hastily wrapped in a woman's petticoat to give the bundle the appropriate bulk.

'*Cramouille!*' he said, this being the worst word he could think of on short notice. And very appropriate, too, if what he thought had happened really had. He turned on Ian.

'She drugged me and seduced you, and her bloody maid stole in here and took the thing whilst ye had your fat heid buried in her . . . er . . .'

'Charms,' Ian said succinctly, and flashed him a brief, evil grin. 'Ye're only jealous. Where d'ye think they've gone?'

It was the truth, and Jamie abandoned any further recriminations, rising and strapping on his belt, hastily arranging dirk, sword and ax in the process.

'Not to Paris, would be my guess. Come on, we'll ask the ostler.'

The ostler confessed himself at a loss; he'd been the worse for drink in the hay-shed, he said, and if someone had taken two horses from the shelter, he hadn't waked to see it.

'Aye, right,' said Jamie, impatient, and grabbing the man's shirtfront, lifted him off his feet and slammed him into the inn's stone wall. The man's head bounced once off the stones and he sagged in Jamie's grip, still conscious but dazed. Jamie drew his dirk left-handed and pressed the edge of it against the man's weathered throat.

'Try again,' he suggested pleasantly. 'I dinna care about the money they gave you – keep it. I want to know which way they went, and when they left.'

The man tried to swallow, and abandoned the attempt when his Adam's apple hit the edge of the dirk.

'About three hours past moonrise,' he croaked. 'They went toward Bonnes. There's a crossroads no more than three miles from here,' he added, now try-ing urgently to be helpful.

Jamie dropped him with a grunt.

'Aye, fine,' he said in disgust. 'Ian – oh, ye've got them.' For Ian had gone straight for their own horses while he dealt with the ostler, and was already lead-ing one out, bridled, the saddle over his arm. 'I'll settle the bill, then.'

The women hadn't made off with his purse, that was something. Either Rebekah bat-Leah Hauberger had some vestige of conscience – which he doubted very much – or she just hadn't thought of it.

It was just past dawn; the women had perhaps six hours' lead.

'Do we believe the ostler?' Ian asked, settling himself in the saddle.

Jamie dug in his purse, pulled out a copper penny and flipped it, catching it on the back of his hand.

'Tails we do, heads we don't?' He took his hand away and peered at the coin. 'Heads.'

'Aye, but the road back is straight all the way through Yvrac,' Ian pointed out. 'And it's nay more than three miles to the crossroads, he said. Whatever ye want to say about the lass, she's no a fool.'

Jamie considered that one for a moment, then nodded. Rebekah couldn't have been sure how much lead she'd have — and unless she'd been lying about her ability to ride (which he wouldn't put past her, but such things weren't easy to fake and she was gey clumsy in the saddle), she'd want to reach a place where the trail could be lost before her pursuers could catch up with her. Besides, the ground was still damp with dew; there might be a chance . . .

'Aye, come on, then.'

Luck was with them. No one had passed the inn during the late night watches, and while the roadbed was trampled with hoofmarks, the recent prints of the women's horses showed clear, edges still crumbling in the damp earth. Once sure they'd got upon the track, the men galloped for the cross-roads, hoping to reach it before other travelers obscured the marks.

No such luck. Farm wagons were already on the move, loaded with produce headed for Parcoul or LacRoche-Chalais, and the crossroad was a maze of ruts and hoofprints. But Jamie had the bright thought of sending Ian down the road that lay toward Parcoul, while he took the one toward La Roche-Chalais, catching up the incoming wagons and questioning the drivers. Within an hour, Ian came pelting back with the news that the women had been seen, riding slowly and cursing volubly at each other, toward Parcoul.

'And *that*,' he said, panting for breath, 'is not all.'

'Aye? Well, tell me while we ride.'

Ian did. He'd been hurrying back to find Jamie, when he'd met Josef-from-Alsace just short of the crossroads, come in search of them.

'D'Eglise was held up near Poitiers,' Ian reported in a shout. 'The same band of men that attacked us at Marmande — Alexandre and Raoul both recognized some of them. Jewish bandits.'

Jamie was shocked, and slowed for a moment to let Ian catch him up.

'Did they get the dowry money?'

'No, but they had a hard fight. Three men

wounded badly enough to need a surgeon, and Paul Martan lost two fingers of his left hand. D'Eglise pulled them into Poitiers, and sent Josef to see if all was well wi' us.'

Jamie's heart bounced into his throat. 'Jesus. Did ye tell him what happened?'

'I did not,' Ian said tersely. 'I told him we'd had an accident wi' the coach, and ye'd gone ahead with the women; I was comin' back to fetch something left behind.'

'Aye, good.' Jamie's heart dropped back into his chest. The last thing he wanted was to have to tell the Captain that they'd lost the girl and the Torah scroll. And he'd be damned if he would.

They traveled fast, stopping only to ask questions now and then, and by the time they pounded into the village of Aubeterre-sur-Dronne, were sure that their quarry lay no more than an hour ahead of them – if the women had passed on through the village.

'Oh, those two?' said a woman, pausing in the act of scrubbing her steps. She stood up slowly, stretching her back. 'I saw them, yes. They rode right by me, and went down the lane there.' She pointed.

'I thank you, Madame,' Jamie said, in his best Parisian French. 'What lies down that lane, please?'

She looked surprised that they didn't know, and frowned a little at such ignorance.

'Why, the chateau of the Vicomte Beaumont, to be sure!'

'To be sure,' Jamie repeated, smiling at her, and Ian saw a dimple appear in her cheek in reply. *'Merci beaucoup, Madame!'*

◦

'What the devil . . . ?' Ian murmured. Jamie reined up beside him, pausing to look at the place. It was a small manor-house, somewhat run-down, but pretty in its bones. And the last place anyone would think to look for a runaway Jewess, he'd say that for it.

'What shall we do now, d'ye think?' he asked, and Jamie shrugged and kicked his horse.

'Go knock on the door and ask, I suppose.'

Ian followed his friend up to the door, feeling intensely conscious of his grubby clothes, sprouting beard, and general state of uncouthness. Such concerns vanished, though, when Jamie's forceful knock was answered.

'Good day, gentlemen!' said the yellow-haired bugger he'd last seen locked in combat in the road-bed with Jamie the day before. The man smiled broadly at them, cheerful despite an obvious black eye and a freshly-split lip. He was dressed in the height of fashion, in a plum-velvet suit, his hair was curled and powdered, and his yellow beard was neatly trimmed. 'I hoped we would see you again. Welcome to my home!' he said, stepping back and raising his hand in a gesture of invitation.

'I thank you, Monsieur ...?' Jamie said slowly, giving Ian a sidelong glance. Ian lifted one shoulder in the ghost of a shrug. Did they have a choice?

The yellow-haired bugger bowed. 'Pierre Robert Heriveaux d'Anton, Vicomte Beaumont, by the grace of the Almighty, for one more day. And you, gentlemen?'

'James Alexander Malcolm MacKenzie Fraser,' Jamie said, with a good attempt at matching the other's grand manner. Only Ian would have noticed the faint hesitation, or the slight tremor in his voice when he added, 'Laird of Broch Tuarach.'

'Ian Alastair Robert MacLeod Murray,' Ian said, with a curt nod, and straightened his shoulders. 'His ... er ... the laird's ... tacksman.'

'Come in, please, gentlemen.' The yellow-haired bugger's eyes shifted just a little, and Ian heard the crunch of gravel behind them, an instant before he felt the prick of a dagger in the small of his back. No, they didn't have a choice.

Inside, they were relieved of their weapons, then escorted down a wide hallway and into a commodious parlor. The wallpaper was faded, and the furniture was good but shabby. By contrast, the big Turkey carpet on the floor glowed like it was woven from jewels. A big roundish thing in the middle was green and gold and red, and concentric circles with wiggly edges surrounded it in waves of blue and red and cream, bordered in a soft, deep red, and the whole of it so ornamented with unusual shapes it would take you a day to look at them all. He'd been so taken with it the first time he saw it, he'd spent a quarter of an hour looking at them, before Big Georges caught him at it and shouted at him to roll the thing up, they hadn't all day.

'Where did ye get this?' Ian asked abruptly, interrupting something the Vicomte was saying to the two rough-clad men who'd taken their weapons.

'What? Oh, the carpet! Yes, isn't it wonderful?' The Vicomte beamed at him, quite unself-conscious, and gestured the two roughs away toward the wall. 'It's part of my wife's dowry.'

'Your wife,' Jamie repeated carefully. He darted a sideways glance at Ian, who took the cue.

'That would be Mademoiselle Hauberger, would it?' he asked. The Vicomte blushed – actually blushed – and Ian realized that the man was no older than he and Jamie were.

'Well. It – we – we have been betrothed for some time, and in Jewish custom, that is almost like being married.'

'Betrothed,' Jamie echoed again. 'Since . . . when, exactly?'

The Vicomte sucked in his lower lip, contemplating them. But whatever caution he might have had was overwhelmed in what were plainly very high spirits.

'Four years,' he said. And unable to contain himself, he beckoned them to a table near the window, and proudly showed them a fancy document, covered with colored scrolly sorts of things and written in some very odd language that was all slashes and tilted lines.

'This is our *ketubah*,' he said, pronouncing the word very carefully. 'Our marriage contract.'

Jamie bent over to peer closely at it.

'Aye, verra nice,' he said politely. 'I see it's no been signed yet. The marriage hasna taken place, then?' Ian saw Jamie's eyes flick over the desk, and could see him passing the possibilities through his mind: Grab the letter-opener off the desk and take the Vicomte hostage? Then find the sly wee bitch, roll her up in one of the smaller rugs and carry her to Paris? That would doubtless be Ian's job, he thought.

A slight movement as one of the roughs shifted his weight caught Ian's eye and he thought, '*Don't do it, eejit!*' at Jamie, as hard as he could. For once, the message seemed to get through; Jamie's shoulders relaxed a little and he straightened up.

'Ye do ken the lass is meant to be marrying some-one else?' he asked baldly. 'I wouldna put it past her not to tell ye.'

The Vicomte's color became higher.

'Certainly I know!' he snapped. 'She was promised to me first, by her father!'

'How long have ye been a Jew?' Jamie asked care-fully, edging round the table. 'I dinna think ye were born to it. I mean — ye *are* a Jew now, aye? For I kent one or two, in Paris, and it's my understanding that they dinna marry people who aren't Jewish.' His eyes flicked round the solid, handsome room. 'It's my understanding that they mostly aren't aristocrats, either.'

The Vicomte was quite red in the face by now. With a sharp word, he sent the roughs out — though they were disposed to argue. While the brief discus-sion was going on, Ian edged closer to Jamie and whispered rapidly to him about the rug in *Gaidhlig*.

'Holy God,' Jamie muttered in the same language. 'I didna see him or either of those two at Marmande, did you?'

Ian had no time to reply and merely shook his head, as the roughs reluctantly acquiesced to Vicomte Pierre's imperious orders and shuffled out with nar-rowed eyes aimed at Ian and Jamie. One of them had Jamie's dirk in his hand, and drew this slowly across his neck in a meaningful gesture as he left.

Aye, they might manage in a fight, he thought, returning the slit-eyed glare, *but not that wee velvet gomerel*. Captain D'Eglise wouldn't have taken on the Vicomte, and neither would a band of professional highwaymen, Jewish or not.

'All right,' the Vicomte said abruptly, leaning his fists on the desk. 'I'll tell you.'

And he did. Rebekah's mother, the daughter of Doctor Hasdi, had fallen in love with a Christian man, and run away with him. The Doctor had declared his daughter dead, as was the usual way in such a situation, and done formal mourning for her. But she was his only child, and he had not been able to forget her. He had arranged to have information brought to him, and knew about Rebekah's birth.

'Then her mother died. That's when I met her – about that time, I mean. Her father was a judge, and my father knew him. She was fourteen and I sixteen; I fell in love with her. And she with me,' he added, giving the Scots a hard eye, as though daring them to disbelieve it. 'We were betrothed, with her father's blessing. But then her father caught a flux and died in two days. And –'

'And her grandfather took her back,' Jamie finished. 'And she became a Jew?'

'By Jewish belief, she was born Jewish; it descends through the mother's line. And ... her mother had told her, privately, about her lost heritage.

She embraced it, once she went to live with her grandfather.'

Ian stirred, and cocked a cynical eyebrow. 'Aye? Why did ye not convert then, if ye're willing to do it now?'

'I said I would!' the Vicomte had one fist curled round his letter-opener as though he would strangle it. 'The miserable old wretch said he did not believe me. He thought I would not give up my – my – this life.' He waved a hand dismissively around the room, encompassing, presumably, his title and property, both of which would be confiscated by the government the moment his conversion became known.

'He said it would be a sham conversion and the moment I had her, I would become a Christian again, and force Rebekah to be Christian, too. Like her father,' he added darkly.

Despite the situation, Ian was beginning to have some sympathy for the wee popinjay. It was a very romantic tale, and he was partial to those. Jamie, however, was still reserving judgement. He gestured at the rug beneath their feet.

'Her dowry, ye said?'

'Yes,' said the Vicomte, but sounded much less certain. 'She says it belonged to her mother. She had some men bring it here last week, along with a chest and a few other things. Anyway,' he said, resuming his self-confidence and glowering at them, 'when the old beast arranged her marriage to that fellow in Paris, I made up my mind to – to –'

'To abduct her. By arrangement, aye? Mmphm,' Jamie said, making a noise indicating his opinion of the Vicomte's skills as a highwayman. He raised one red brow at Pierre's black eye, but forebore to make any more remarks, thank God. It hadn't escaped Ian that they were prisoners, though it maybe had Jamie.

'May we speak with Mademoiselle Hauberger?' Ian asked politely. 'Just to make sure she's come of her own free will, aye?'

'Rather plainly, she did, since you followed her here.' The Vicomte hadn't liked Jamie's noise. 'No, you may not. She's busy.' He raised his hands and clapped them sharply, and the rough fellows came back in, along with a half-dozen or so male servants as reinforcement, led by a tall, severe-looking butler, armed with a stout walking-stick.

'Go with Ecrivisse, gentlemen. He'll see to your comfort.'

'Comfort' proved to be the chateau's wine cellar, which was fragrant, but cold. Also dark. The Vicomte's hospitality did not extend so far as a candle.

'If he meant to kill us, he'd have done it already,' Ian reasoned.

'Mmphm.' Jamie sat on the stairs, the fold of his plaid pulled up around his shoulders against the chill. There was music coming from somewhere outside: the faint sound of a fiddle and the tap of a little hand-drum. It started, then stopped, then started again.

Ian wandered restlessly to and fro; it wasn't a very large cellar. If he didn't mean to kill them, what did the Vicomte mean to do with them?

'He's waiting for something to happen,' Jamie said suddenly, answering the thought. 'Something to do wi' the lass, I expect.'

'Aye, reckon.' Ian sat down on the stairs, nudging Jamie over. '*A Dhia*, that's cold!'

'Mm,' said Jamie absently. 'Maybe they mean to run. If so, I hope he leaves someone behind to let us out, and doesna mean to leave us here to starve.'

'We wouldna starve,' Ian pointed out logically. 'We could live on wine for a good long time. Someone would come, before it ran out.' He paused a moment, trying to imagine what it would be like to stay drunk for several weeks.

'That's a thought.' Jamie got up, a little stiff from the cold, and went off to rummage the racks. There was no light to speak of, save what seeped through the crack at the bottom of the door to the cellar, but Ian could hear Jamie pulling out bottles and sniffing the corks.

He came back in a bit with a bottle, and sitting down again, drew the cork with his teeth and spat it to one side. He took a sip, then another, then tilted back the bottle for a generous swig, and handed it to Ian.

'No bad,' he said.

It wasn't, and there wasn't much conversation for the next little while. Eventually, though, Jamie set the empty bottle down, belched gently, and said, 'It's her.'

'What's her? Rebekah, ye mean. I daresay.' Then after a moment, 'What's her?'

'It's her,' Jamie repeated. 'Ken what the Jew said – Ephraim bar-Sefer? About how his gang knew where to strike, because they got information from some outside source? It's her. She told them.'

Jamie spoke with such certainty that Ian was staggered for a moment, but then marshaled his wits.

'That wee lass? Granted, she put one over on us – and I suppose she at least kent about Pierre's abduction, but . . .'

Jamie snorted.

'Aye, Pierre. Does the mannie strike ye either as a criminal or a great schemer?'

'No, but –'

'Does she?'

'Well . . .'

'Exactly.'

Jamie got up and wandered off into the racks

again, this time returning with what smelled to Ian like one of the very good local red wines. It was like drinking his mam's strawberry preserves on toast with a cup of strong tea, he thought approvingly.

'Besides,' Jamie went on, as though there'd been no interruption in his train of thought, 'd'ye recall what the maid said to her? When I got my heid half-stove in? "Perhaps he's been killed. How would you feel then?" Nay, she'd planned the whole thing – to have Pierre and his lads stop the coach and make away with the women and the scroll, and doubtless Monsieur Pickle, too. *But –*' he added, sticking up a finger in front of Ian's face to stop him interrupting, 'then Josef-from-Alsace tells ye that thieves – and the *same* thieves as before, or some of them – attacked the band wi' the dowry money. Ye ken well, that canna have been Pierre. It had to be her who told them.'

Ian was forced to admit the logic of this. Pierre had enthusiasm, but couldn't possibly be considered a professional highwayman.

'But a lass . . .' he said, helplessly. 'How could she –'
Jamie grunted.

'D'Eglise said Doctor Hasdi's a man much respected among the Jews of Bordeaux. And plainly he's kent as far as Paris, or how else did he make the match for his grand-daughter? But he doesna speak French. Want to bet me that she didna manage his correspondence?'

'No,' Ian said, and took another swallow. 'Mmphm.'

Some minutes later, he said, 'That rug. And the other things Monsieur le Vicomte mentioned – her *dowry*.'

Jamie made an approving noise.

'Aye. Her percentage of the take, more like. Ye can see our lad Pierre hasna got much money, and he'd lose all his property when he converted. She was feathering their nest, like – makin' sure they'd have enough to live on. Enough to live *well* on.'

'Well, then,' Ian said, after a moment's silence. 'There ye are.'

~

The afternoon dragged on. After the second bottle, they agreed to drink no more for the time being, in case a clear head should be necessary if or when the door at last opened, and aside from going off now and then to have a pee behind the furthest wine-racks, they stayed huddled on the stairs.

Jamie was singing softly along to the fiddle's distant tune, when the door finally *did* open. He stopped abruptly, and lunged awkwardly to his feet, nearly falling, his knees stiff with cold.

'Monsieurs?' said the butler, peering down at them. 'If you will be so kind as to follow me, please?'

To their surprise, the butler led them straight out

of the house, and down a small path, in the direction of the distant music. The air outside was fresh and wonderful after the must of the cellar, and Jamie filled his lungs with it, wondering what the devil . . . ?

Then they rounded a bend in the path and saw a garden court before them, lit by torches driven into the ground. Somewhat overgrown, but with a fountain tinkling away in the center – and just by the fountain, a sort of canopy, its cloth glimmering pale in the dusk. There was a little knot of people standing near it, talking, and as the butler paused, holding them back with one hand, Vicomte Pierre broke away from the group and came toward them, smiling.

'My apologies for the inconvenience, gentlemen,' he said, a huge smile splitting his face. He looked drunk, but Jamie thought he wasn't – no smell of spirits. 'Rebekah had to prepare herself. And we wanted to wait for nightfall.'

'To do what?' Ian asked suspiciously, and the Vicomte giggled. Jamie didn't mean to wrong the man, but it was a giggle. He gave Ian an eye and Ian gave it back. Aye, it was a giggle.

'To be married,' Pierre said, and while his voice was still full of *joie de vivre*, he said the words with a sense of deep reverence that struck Jamie somewhere in the chest. Pierre turned and waved a hand toward the darkening sky, where the stars were beginning to prick and sparkle. 'For luck, you know — that our descendants may be as numerous as the stars.'

'Mmphm,' Jamie said politely.

'But come with me, if you will.' Pierre was already striding back to the knot of . . . well, Jamie supposed they must be wedding guests . . . beckoning to the Scots to follow.

Marie the maid was there, along with a few other women; she gave Jamie and Ian a wary look. But it was the men with whom the Vicomte was concerned. He spoke a few words to his guests, and three men came back with him, all dressed formally, if somewhat oddly, with little velvet skullcaps decorated with beads, and enormous beards.

'May I present Monsieur Gershom Ackerman, and Monsieur Levi Champfleur. Our witnesses. And Reb Cohen, who will officiate.'

The men shook hands, murmuring politeness. Jamie and Ian exchanged looks. Why were *they* here?

The Vicomte caught the look and interpreted it correctly.

'I wish you to return to Doctor Hasdi,' he said, the effervescence in his voice momentarily supplanted by a note of steel. 'And tell him that everything — everything! — was done in accordance with proper custom and according to the Law. This marriage will not be undone. By anyone.'

'Mmphm,' said Ian, less politely.

And so it was that a few minutes later, they found themselves standing among the male wedding guests — the women stood on the other side of the canopy — watching as Rebekah came down the path, jingling faintly. She wore a dress of deep red silk; Jamie could see the torchlight shift and shimmer through its folds as she moved. There were gold bracelets on both wrists, and she had a veil over her head and face, with a little headdress sort of thing made of gold chains that dipped across her forehead, strung with little medallions and bells — it was this that made the jingling sound. It reminded him of the Torah scroll, and he stiffened a little at the thought.

Pierre stood with the rabbi under the canopy; as she approached, he stepped apart, and she came to him. She didn't touch him, though, but proceeded to walk round him. And round him, and round him. Seven times she circled him, and the hairs rose a little on the back of Jamie's neck; it had the faint sense of magic about it — or witchcraft. Something she did, binding the man.

She came face-to-face with Jamie as she made each turn and plainly could see him in the light of the torches, but her eyes were fixed straight ahead; she made no acknowledgement of anyone — not even Pierre.

But then the circling was done and she came to stand by his side. The rabbi said a few words of welcome to the guests, and then turning to the bride and groom, poured out a cup of wine, said what appeared to be a Hebrew blessing over it. Jamie made out the beginning . . . *'Blessed are you, Adonai our God . . . '* but then lost the thread.

Pierre reached into his pocket when Reb Cohen stopped speaking, took out a small object – clearly a ring – and taking Rebekah's hand in his, put it on the forefinger of her right hand, smiling down into her face with a tenderness that, despite everything, rather caught at Jamie's heart. Then Pierre lifted her veil, and he caught a glimpse of the answering tenderness on Rebekah's face in the instant before her husband kissed her.

The congregation sighed as one.

The rabbi picked up a sheet of parchment from a little table nearby. The thing he'd called a *ketubah*, Jamie saw – the wedding contract.

The rabbi read the thing out, first in a language Jamie didn't recognize, and then again in French. It wasn't so different from the few marriage contracts he'd seen, laying out the disposition of property and what was due to the bride and all . . . though he noted with disapproval that it provided for the possibility of divorce. His attention wandered a bit then;

Rebekah's face glowed in the torchlight like pearl and ivory and the roundness of her bosom showed clearly as she breathed. In spite of everything he thought he now knew about her, he experienced a brief wave of envy toward Pierre.

The contract read and carefully laid aside, the rabbi recited a string of blessings; he kent it was blessings because he caught the words 'Blessed are you, Adonai . . .' over and over, though the subject of the blessings seemed to be everything from the congregation to Jerusalem, so far as he could tell. The bride and groom had another sip of wine.

A pause then, and Jamie expected some official word from the rabbi, uniting husband and wife, but it didn't come. Instead, one of the witnesses took the wine glass, wrapped it in a linen napkin, and placed it on the ground in front of Pierre. To the Scots' astonishment, he promptly stamped on the thing — and the crowd burst into applause.

For a few moments, everything seemed quite like a country wedding, with everyone crowding round, wanting to congratulate the happy couple. But within moments, the happy couple was moving off toward the house, while the guests all streamed toward tables that had been set up at the far side of the garden, laden with food and drink.

'Come on,' Jamie muttered, and caught Ian by the arm. They hastened after the newly-wedded pair, Ian demanding to know what the devil Jamie thought he was doing?

⁓

'I want to talk to her — alone. You stop him, keep him talking for as long as ye can.'

'I — how?'

'How would I know? Ye'll think of something.' They had reached the house, and ducking in close upon Pierre's heels, he saw that by good luck, the man had stopped to say something to a servant. Rebekah was just vanishing down a long hallway; he saw her put her hand to a door.

'The best of luck to ye, man!' he said, clapping Pierre so heartily on the shoulder that the groom staggered. Before he could recover, Ian, very obviously commending his soul to God, stepped up and seized him by the hand, which he wrang vigorously, meanwhile giving Jamie a private, 'Hurry the bloody hell *up!*' sort of look.

Grinning, Jamie ran down the short hallway to the door where he'd seen Rebekah disappear. The grin disappeared as his hand touched the doorknob, though, and the face he presented to her as he entered was as grim as he could make it.

Her eyes widened in shock and indignation at the sight of him.

'What are you doing here? No one is supposed to come in here but me and my husband!'

'He's on his way,' Jamie assured her. 'The question is – will he get here?'

Her little fist curled up in a way that would have been comical, if he didn't know as much about her as he did.

'Is that a threat?' she said, in a tone as incredulous as it was menacing. 'Here? You dare threaten me *here*?'

'Aye, I do. I want that scroll.'

'Well, you're not getting it,' she snapped. He saw her glance flicker over the table, probably in search either of a bell to summon help, or something to bash him on the head with, but the table held nothing but a platter of stuffed rolls and exotic sweeties. There *was* a bottle of wine, and he saw her eye light on that with calculation, but he stretched out a long arm and got hold of it before she could.

'I dinna want it for myself,' he said. 'I mean to take it back to your grandfather.'

'Him?' Her face hardened. 'No. It's worth more to him than *I* am,' she added bitterly, 'but at least that means I can use it for protection. As long as I have it, he won't try to hurt Pierre or drag me back, for fear I might damage it. I'm keeping it.'

'I think he'd be a great deal better off without ye, and doubtless he kens that fine,' Jamie informed her, and had to harden himself against the sudden look of hurt in her eyes. He supposed even spiders might have feelings, but that was neither here nor there.

'Where's Pierre?' she demanded, rising to her feet. 'If you've harmed a hair on his head, I'll –'

'I wouldna touch the poor gomerel and neither would Ian – Juan, I mean. When I said the question was whether he got to ye or not, I meant whether he thinks better of his bargain.'

'What?' He thought she paled a little, but it was hard to tell.

'You give me the scroll to take back to your grandfather – a wee letter of apology to go with it wouldna come amiss, but I willna insist on that – or Ian and I take Pierre out back and have a frank word regarding his new wife.'

'Tell him what you like!' she snapped. 'He wouldn't believe any of your made-up tales!'

'Oh, aye? And if I tell him exactly what happened to Efraim bar-Sefer? And why?'

'Who?' she said, but now she really had gone pale to the lips, and put out a hand to the table to steady herself.

'Do ye ken yourself what happened to him? No? Well, I'll tell ye, lass.' And he did so, with a terse brutality that made her sit down suddenly, tiny pearls of sweat appearing round the gold medallions that hung across her forehead.

'Pierre already kens at least a bit about your wee gang, I think – but maybe not what a ruthless, grasping wee besom ye really are.'

'It wasn't me! I didn't kill Efraim!'

'If not for you, he'd no be dead, and I reckon Pierre would see that. I can tell him where the body is,' he added, more delicately. 'I buried the man myself.'

Her lips were pressed so hard together that nothing showed but a straight white line.

'Ye havena got long,' he said, quietly now, but keeping his eyes on hers. 'Ian canna hold him off much longer, and if he comes in – then I tell him everything, in front of you, and ye do what ye can then to persuade him I'm a liar.'

She stood up abruptly, her chains and bracelets all a-jangle, and stamped to the door of the inner room. She flung it open, and Marie jerked back, shocked.

Rebekah said something to her in Ladino, sharp, and with a small gasp, the maid scurried off.

'All *right*,' Rebekah said through gritted teeth, turning back to him. 'Take it and be damned, you *dog*.'

'Indeed I will, ye bloody wee bitch,' he replied with great politeness. Her hand closed round a stuffed roll, but instead of throwing it at him, she merely squeezed it into paste and crumbs, slapping the remains back on the tray with a small exclamation of fury.

The sweet chiming of the Torah scroll presaged

Marie's hasty arrival, the precious thing clasped in her arms. She glanced at her mistress, and at Rebekah's curt nod, delivered it with great reluctance into the arms of the Christian dog.

Jamie bowed, first to maid and then mistress, and backed toward the door.

'*Shalom*,' he said, and closed the door an instant before the silver platter hit it with a ringing thud.

'Did it hurt a lot?' Ian was asking Pierre with interest, when Jamie came up to them.

'My God, you have no idea,' Pierre replied fervently. 'But it was worth it.' He divided a beaming smile between Ian and Jamie and bowed to them, not even noticing the canvas-wrapped bundle in Jamie's arms. 'You must excuse me, gentlemen; my bride awaits me!'

'Did what hurt a lot?' Jamie inquired, leading the way hastily out through a side door. No point in attracting attention, after all.

'Ye ken he was born a Christian, but converted in order to marry the wee besom,' Ian said. 'So he had to be circumcised.' He crossed himself at the thought, and Jamie laughed.

'What is it they call the stick-insect things where the female one bites off the head of the male one after he's got the business started?' he asked, nudging the door open with his bum.

Ian's brow creased for an instant.

'Praying mantis, I think. Why?'

'I think our wee friend Pierre may have a more interesting wedding night than he expects. Come on.'

Bordeaux

It wasn't the worst thing he'd ever had to do, but he wasn't looking forward to it. Jamie paused outside the gate of Doctor Hasdi's house, the Torah scroll in its wrappings in his arms. Ian was looking a bit worm-eaten, and Jamie reckoned he kent why. Having to tell the Doctor what had happened to his grand-daughter was one thing; telling him to his face with the knowledge of what said granddaughter's nipples felt like fresh in the mind . . . or the hand . . .

'Ye dinna have to come in, man,' he said to Ian. 'I can do it alone.'

Ian's mouth twitched, but he shook his head and stepped up next to Jamie.

'On your right, man,' he said, simply. Jamie smiled. When he'd been five years old, Ian's da, Auld John, had persuaded his own Da to let Jamie handle a sword cack-handed, as he was wont to do. 'And you, lad,' he'd said to Ian, very serious, 'it's your duty to stand on your laird's right hand, and guard his weak side.'

'Aye,' Jamie said. 'Right, then.' And rang the bell.

Afterward, they wandered slowly through the streets of Bordeaux, making their way toward nothing in particular, not speaking much.

Doctor Hasdi had received them courteously, though with a look of mingled horror and apprehension on his face when he saw the scroll. This look had faded to one of relief at hearing – the man-servant had had enough French to interpret for them – that his grand-daughter was safe, then to shock, and finally to a set expression that Jamie couldn't read. Was it anger, sadness, resignation?

When Jamie had finished the story, they sat uneasily, not sure what to do next. Doctor Hasdi sat at his desk, head bowed, his hands resting gently on the scroll. Finally, he raised his head, and nodded to them both, one and then the other. His face was calm now, giving nothing away.

'Thank you,' he said in heavily-accented French. '*Shalom.*'

'Are ye hungry?' Ian motioned toward a small boulangerie whose trays bore filled rolls and big, fragrant round loaves. He was starving himself, though half an hour ago, his wame had been in knots.

'Aye, maybe.' Jamie kept walking, though, and Ian shrugged and followed.

'What d'ye think the Captain will do when we tell him?' Ian wasn't all that bothered. There was always work for a good-sized man who kent what to do with a sword. And he owned his own weapons. They'd have to buy Jamie a sword, though. Everything he was wearing, from pistols to ax, belonged to D'Eglise.

He was busy enough calculating the cost of a decent sword against what remained of their pay that he didn't notice Jamie not answering him. He did notice that his friend was walking faster, though, and hurrying to catch up, he saw what they were heading for. The tavern where the pretty brown-haired barmaid had taken Jamie for a Jew.

Oh, like that, is it? he thought, and hid a grin. Aye, well, there was one sure way the lad could prove to the lass that he wasn't a Jew.

The place was moiling when they walked in, and not in a good way; Ian sensed it instantly. There were soldiers there, army soldiers, and other fighting-men, mercenaries like themselves, and no love wasted between them. You could cut the air with a knife, and judging from a splotch of half-dried blood on the floor, somebody had already tried.

There were women, but fewer than before, and the barmaids kept their eyes on their trays, not flirting tonight.

Jamie wasn't taking heed of the atmosphere; Ian could see him looking round for her; the brown-haired lass wasn't on the floor. They might have asked after her – if they'd known her name.

'Upstairs, maybe?' Ian said, leaning in to half-shout into Jamie's ear over the noise. Jamie nodded and began forging through the crowd, Ian bobbing in his wake, hoping they found the lass quickly, so he could eat whilst Jamie got on with it.

The stairs were crowded – with men coming down. Something was amiss up there, and Jamie shoved someone into the wall with a thump, pushing past. Some nameless anxiety shot jolts down his spine, and he was half-prepared before he pushed through a little knot of onlookers at the head of the stairs and saw them.

Big Mathieu, and the brown-haired girl. There was a big open room here, with a hallway lined with tiny cubicles leading back from it; Mathieu had the girl by the arm and was boosting her toward the hallway with a hand on her bum, despite her protests.

'Let go of her!' Jamie said, not shouting, but raising his voice well enough to be heard easily. Mathieu paid not the least attention, though everyone else turned to look at Jamie, startled.

He heard Ian mutter, 'Joseph, Mary and Bride preserve us,' behind him, but paid no heed. He covered the distance to Mathieu in three strides, and kicked him in the arse.

He ducked, by reflex, but Mathieu merely turned and gave him a hot eye, ignoring the whoops and guffaws from the spectators.

'Later, little boy,' he said. 'I'm busy now.'

He scooped the young woman into one big arm and kissed her sloppily, rubbing his stubbled face hard over hers, so she squealed and pushed at him to get away.

Jamie drew the pistol from his belt.

'I said, let her go.' The noise dropped suddenly, but he barely noticed, for the roaring of blood in his ears.

Mathieu turned his head, incredulous. Then snorted with contempt, grinned unpleasantly, and shoved the girl into the wall so her head struck with a thump, pinning her there with his bulk.

The pistol was primed.

'*Salop!*' Jamie roared. 'Don't touch her! Let her go!'

He clenched his teeth and aimed with both hands, rage and fright making his hands tremble.

Mathieu didn't even look at him. The big man half turned away, a casual hand on her breast. She squealed as he twisted it, and Jamie fired. Mathieu whirled, the pistol he'd had concealed in his own belt now in hand, and the air shattered in an explosion of sound and white smoke.

There were shouts of alarm, excitement — and another pistol went off, somewhere behind Jamie. *Ian?* He thought dimly, but no, Ian was running toward Mathieu, leaping for the massive arm rising, the second pistol's barrel making circles as Mathieu struggled to fix it on Jamie. It discharged, and the ball hit one of the lanterns that stood on the tables, which exploded with a *whuff* and a bloom of flame.

Jamie had reversed his pistol and was hammering at Mathieu's head with the butt before he was conscious of having crossed the room. Mathieu's mad-boar eyes were almost invisible, slitted with the glee of fighting, and the sudden curtain of blood that fell over his face did nothing but enhance his grin, blood running down between his teeth. He shook Ian off with a shove that sent him crashing into the wall, then wrapped one big arm almost casually around Jamie's body, and with a snap of his head, butted him in the face.

Jamie had turned his head reflexively and thus

avoided a broken nose, but the impact crushed the flesh of his jaw into his teeth and his mouth filled with blood. His head was spinning with the force of the blow, but he got a hand under Mathieu's jaw and shoved upward with all his strength, trying to break the man's neck. His hand slipped off the sweat-greased flesh, though and Mathieu let go his grip in order to try to knee Jamie in the stones. A knee like a cannonball struck him a numbing blow in the thigh as he squirmed free, and he staggered, grabbing Mathieu's arm just as Ian came dodging in from the side, seizing the other. Without a moment's hesitation, Mathieu's huge forearms twisted; he seized the Scots by the scruffs of their necks and cracked their heads together.

Jamie couldn't see and could barely move, but kept moving anyway, groping blindly. He was on the floor, could feel boards, wetness . . . his pawing hand struck flesh and he lunged forward and bit Mathieu as hard as he could in the calf of the leg. Fresh blood filled his mouth, hotter than his own and he gagged but kept his teeth locked in the hairy flesh, clinging stubbornly as the leg he clung to kicked in frenzy. His ears were ringing, he was vaguely aware of screaming and shouting, but it didn't matter.

Something had come upon him and nothing mattered. Some small remnant of his consciousness registered surprise, and then that was gone, too. No pain, no thought. He was a red thing and while he saw things, faces, blood, bits of room, they didn't matter. Blood took him, and when some sense of himself came back, he was kneeling astride the man, hands locked around the big man's neck, hands throbbing with a pounding pulse, his or his victim's, he couldn't tell.

Him. Him. He'd lost the man's name. His eyes were bulging, the ragged mouth slobbered and gaped, and there was a small, sweet *crack* as something broke under Jamie's thumbs. He squeezed with all he had, squeezed and squeezed and felt the huge body beneath him go strangely limp.

He went on squeezing, couldn't stop, until a hand seized him by the arm and shook him, hard.

'Stop,' a voice croaked, hot in his ear. 'Jamie. Stop.'

He blinked up at the white, bony face, unable to put a name to it. Then drew breath — the first he could remember drawing for some time — and with it came a thick stink, blood and shit and reeking sweat, and he became suddenly aware of the horrible spongy feeling of the body he was sitting on. He scrambled awkwardly off, sprawling on the floor as his muscles spasmed and trembled.

Then he saw her.

She was lying crumpled against the wall, curled into herself, her brown hair spilling across the boards. He got to his knees, crawling to her.

He was making a small whimpering noise, trying to talk, having no words. Got to the wall and gathered her into his arms, limp, her head lolling, striking his shoulder, her hair soft against his face, smelling of smoke and her own sweet musk.

'*A nighean,*' he managed. 'Christ, *a nighean.* Are ye . . .'

'Jesus,' said a voice by his side, and he felt the vibration as Ian – thank God, the name had come back, of course it was Ian – collapsed next to him. His friend had a blood-stained dirk still clutched in his hand. 'Oh, Jesus, Jamie.'

He looked up, puzzled, desperate, and then looked down as the girl's body slipped from his grasp and fell back across his knees with impossible boneless grace, the small dark hole in her white breast stained with only a little blood. Not much at all.

He'd made Jamie come with him to the cathedral of St Andre, and insisted he go to confession. Jamie had balked – no great surprise.

'No. I can't.'

'We'll go together.' Ian had taken him firmly by the arm and very literally dragged him over the threshold. Once inside, he was counting on the atmosphere of the place to keep Jamie there.

His friend stopped dead, the whites of his eyes showing as he glanced warily around.

The stone vault of the ceiling soared into shadow overhead, but pools of colored light from the stained-glass windows lay soft on the worn slates of the aisle.

'I shouldna be here,' Jamie muttered under his breath.

'Where better, eejit? Come on,' Ian muttered back, and pulled Jamie down the side aisle to the chapel of Saint Estephe. Most of the side-chapels were lavishly furnished, monuments to the importance of wealthy families. This one was a tiny, undecorated stone alcove, containing little more than an altar, a faded tapestry of a faceless saint, and a small stand where candles could be placed.

'Stay here.' Ian planted Jamie dead in front of the altar and ducked out, going to buy a candle from the old woman who sold them near the main door. He'd changed his mind about trying to make Jamie go to confession; he knew fine when ye could get a Fraser to do something, and when ye couldn't.

He worried a bit that Jamie would leave, and hurried back to the chapel, but Jamie was still there, standing in the middle of the tiny space, head down, staring at the floor.

'Here, then,' Ian said, pulling him toward the altar.

He plunked the candle – an expensive one, beeswax and large – on the stand, and pulled the paper spill the old lady had given him out of his sleeve, offering it to Jamie. 'Light it. We'll say a prayer for your Da. And . . . and for her.'

He could see tears trembling on Jamie's lashes, glittering in the red glow of the sanctuary lamp that hung above the altar, but Jamie blinked them back and firmed his jaw.

'All right,' he said, low-voiced, but he hesitated. Ian sighed, took the spill out of his hand, and standing on tip-toe, lit it from the sanctuary lamp.

'Do it,' he whispered, handing it to Jamie, 'or I'll gie ye a good one in the kidney, right here.'

Jamie made a sound that might have been the breath of a laugh, and lowered the lit spill to the candle's wick. The fire rose up, a pure high flame with blue at its heart, then settled as Jamie pulled the spill away and shook it out in a plume of smoke.

They stood for some time, hands clasped loosely in front of them, watching the candle burn. Ian prayed for his mam and da, his sister and her bairns . . . with some hesitation (was it proper to pray for a Jew?), for Rebekah bat-Leah, and with a side-long glance at Jamie, to be sure he wasn't looking, for Jenny Fraser. Then the soul of Brian Fraser . . . and then, eyes tight shut, for the friend beside him.

The sounds of the church faded, the whispering

stones and echoes of wood, the shuffle of feet and the rolling gabble of the pigeons on the roof. Ian stopped saying words, but was still praying. And then that stopped too, and there was only peace, and the soft beating of his heart.

He heard Jamie sigh, from somewhere deep inside, and opened his eyes. Without speaking, they went out, leaving the candle to keep watch.

'Did ye not mean to go to confession yourself?' Jamie asked, stopping near the church's main door. There was a priest in the confessional; two or three people stood a discreet distance away from the carved wooden stall, out of earshot, waiting.

'It'll bide,' Ian said, with a shrug. 'If ye're goin' to Hell, I might as well go, too. God knows, ye'll never manage alone.'

Jamie smiled – a wee bit of a smile, but still – and pushed the door open into sunlight.

They strolled aimlessly for a bit, not talking, and found themselves eventually on the river's edge, watching the Garonne's dark waters flow past, carrying debris from a recent storm.

'It means "peace",' Jamie said at last. 'What he said to me. The Doctor. *"Shalom."*' Ian kent that fine.

'Aye,' he said. 'But peace is no our business now, is it? We're soldiers.' He jerked his chin toward the nearby pier, where a packet-boat rode at anchor. 'I hear the King of Prussia needs a few good men.'

'So he does,' said Jamie, and squared his shoulders. 'Come on, then.'

Author's Note: I would like to acknowledge the help of several people in researching aspects of Jewish history, law and custom for this story: Elle Druskin (author of *To Catch a Cop*), Sarah Meyer (Registered Midwife), Carol Krenz, Celia K. and her Reb Mom, and especially Darlene Marshall (author of *Castaway Dreams*). I'm indebted also to Rabbi Joseph Telushkin's very helpful book, *Jewish Literacy*. Any errors are mine.

Intermezzo

Some books have a Foreword, offering either a welcome or an explanation (or, occasionally, an excuse) for what you're about to read. Others may have a Prologue. This is ostensibly an integral part of the story itself, but many careless readers skip a Prologue, under the assumption that if anything truly important was being said, it would be Chapter One. (This would be a Serious Mistake to make with one of my books, and I strongly encourage you never to do that . . .).

A few books may have an Epilogue, in which the writer takes farewell of the readers, thanks them for their patience, adds a few words about things that may have happened after the story ended, but for which there wasn't time — or, perhaps, uses that brief space for the purpose of deliberately confusing or puzzling the readers, but I'm sure we don't personally know anyone who does *that* . . .

I've occasionally written a Foreword for someone else's book (have been honored to do this for Thomas Paine's *Common Sense* and Sir Walter Scott's *Ivanhoe*, and very pleased to do it for friends now and then), but never for my own.

I *do* write Prologues. Mine are neither used to provide set-up information outside the main narrative, nor to introduce mysterious characters whose identity you aren't supposed to know until the end. Each of my Prologues is the voice of that particular book. An image or a brief meditation, an emotional summary, if you will. It's like the wax seal on an 18th century letter; the personal stamp of the sender's signet a promise of secrets about to be revealed.

I've also written the occasional Epilogue, and I will leave it to the readers to discern my motives in doing so.

But I've never written something like this, so you'll have to bear with me. This is basically a description of what you're holding, and an explanation of why you're holding it. (And here you thought you already knew that . . . but wait . . . !)

You probably know what *Outlander* is, whether you've read it or merely seen the television show. It's the first novel in a long and interesting story. But even a long story can't hold everything, and so of latter years, I've taken to writing shorter pieces (I call them 'bulges' – think of a snake digesting a deer ...) that expand upon the lives and times of the people who live in my head.

One of these shorter bits is *Virgins*, which you've just read, and I hope you enjoyed it. You will probably have known who Jamie Fraser was before reading it, but if not, you know now.

Virgins is, therefore, technically a prequel to *Outlander*. This being so, the publisher thought it would be desirable to provide a brief sample of *Outlander*, either for the benefit of people who haven't encountered it in print before, or to refresh the memories of those who have.

I quite agreed – but noted that in fact, Jamie Fraser doesn't enter the story immediately. In fact, *Outlander* begins roughly two centuries after his death (whenever that may happen ... it hasn't yet), and the woman who defines his soul and gives purpose to his life is happily married to someone else. Thinking that this might be slightly confusing to some readers, I suggested that perhaps we should provide a somewhat lengthier excerpt of *Outlander*, in order to make a logical connection between the young mercenary of *Virgins* and the still-young but more experienced (in some areas ...) Scottish outlaw who attracts Claire Randall's notice by bleeding not-quite-to-death in front of her.

That's why you're getting more than the first chapter of *Outlander*, and I hope you'll enjoy all of it, in the fullness of time.

Thank you!

Diana Gabaldon
August 2016

DIANA GABALDON

OUTLANDER

I

A New Beginning

It wasn't a very likely place for disappearances, at
least at first glance. Mrs Baird's was like a thousand
other Highland bed-and-breakfast establishments in
1946; clean and quiet, with fading floral wallpaper,
gleaming floors and a coin-operated water heater in
the bathroom. Mrs Baird herself was squat and easy-
going, and made no objection to Frank lining her
tiny rose-sprigged parlour with the dozens of books
and papers with which he always travelled.

I met Mrs Baird in the front hall on my way out.
She stopped me with a pudgy hand on my arm and
patted at my hair.

'Dear me, Mrs Randall, ye canna go out like that!
Here, just let me tuck that bit in for ye. There! That's
better. Ye know, my cousin was tellin' me about a new

perm she tried, comes out beautiful and holds like a dream; perhaps ye should try that kind next time.'

I hadn't the heart to tell her that the waywardness of my light brown curls was strictly the fault of nature, and not due to any dereliction on the part of the permanent-wave manufacturers. Her own tightly marcelled waves suffered from no such perversity.

'Yes, I'll do that, Mrs Baird,' I lied. 'I'm just going down to meet Frank. We'll be back for tea.' I ducked out of the door and down the path before she could detect any further defects in my undisciplined appearance. After five years as an army nurse, I was enjoying the escape from uniforms by indulging in brightly printed blouses and long skirts, totally unsuited for rough walking through the heather.

Not that I had originally planned to do a lot of that; my thoughts ran more on the lines of sleeping late in the mornings, and long, lazy afternoons in bed with Frank, not sleeping. However, it was difficult to maintain the proper mood of languorous romance with Mrs Baird industriously hoovering away outside our door.

'That must be the dirtiest bit of carpet in the entire Scottish Highlands,' Frank had observed that morning as we lay in bed listening to the ferocious roar of the vacuum in the hallway.

'Nearly as dirty as our landlady's mind,' I agreed. 'Perhaps we should have gone to Brighton after all.'

We had chosen the Highlands as a place to holiday before Frank took up his appointment as a history professor at Oxford, on the grounds that Scotland had been somewhat less touched by the physical horrors of war than the rest of Britain, and was less susceptible to the frenetic postwar gaiety that infected more popular holiday spots.

And without discussing it, I think we both felt that it was a symbolic place to re-establish our marriage; we had been married and spent a two-day honeymoon in the Highlands, shortly before the outbreak of war seven years before. A peaceful refuge in which to rediscover each other, we thought, not realizing that, while golf and fishing are Scotland's most popular outdoor sports, gossip is the most popular indoor sport. And when it rains as much as it does in Scotland, people spend a lot of time indoors.

'Where are you going?' I asked as Frank swung his feet out of bed.

'I'd hate the dear old thing to be disappointed in us,' he answered. Sitting up on the side of the ancient bed he bounced gently up and down, creating a piercing rhythmic squeak. The hoovering in the hall stopped abruptly. After a minute or two of bouncing he gave a loud, theatrical groan and collapsed backwards with a twang of protesting springs. I giggled helplessly into a pillow, so as not to disturb the breathless silence outside.

Frank waggled his eyebrows at me. 'You're supposed to moan ecstatically, not giggle,' he admonished in a whisper. 'She'll think I'm not a good lover.'

'You'll have to keep it up for longer than that if you expect ecstatic moans,' I answered. 'Two minutes doesn't deserve any more than a giggle.'

'Inconsiderate wench. I came here for a rest, remember?'

'Lazybones. You'll never manage the next branch on your family tree unless you show a bit more industry than that.'

Frank's passion for genealogy was yet another reason for choosing the Highlands. According to one of the filthy scraps of paper he lugged to and fro, some tiresome ancestor of his had had something to do with something or other in this region back in the middle of the eighteenth — or was it seventeenth? — century.

'If I end up as a childless stub on my family tree, it will undoubtedly be the fault of our untiring hostess out there. After all, we've been married almost seven years. Little Frank will be quite legitimate without being conceived in the presence of a witness.'

'If he's conceived at all,' I said pessimistically. We had been disappointed yet again the week before leaving for our Highland retreat.

'With all this bracing fresh air and healthy diet? How could we help but manage here?' High tea the night before had been herring, fried. Lunch had been herring, pickled. And the pungent scent now wafting up the stairwell strongly intimated that breakfast was to be herring, kippered.

'Unless you're contemplating an encore performance for the edification of Mrs Baird,' I suggested, 'you'd better get dressed. Aren't you meeting that parson at ten?' The Reverend Mr Reginald Wakefield, minister of the local parish, was to provide some rivetingly fascinating baptismal registers for Frank's inspection, not to mention the glittering prospect that he might have unearthed some mouldering army dispatches or somesuch that mentioned the notorious ancestor.

'What's the name of that six-times-great-grandfather of yours again?' I asked. 'The one who mucked about here during one of the Risings? I can't remember if it was Willy or Walter.'

'Actually, it was Jonathan.' Frank took my complete disinterest in family history placidly, but remained always on guard, ready to seize the slightest expression of inquisitiveness as an excuse for telling me all facts known to date about the early Randalls and their connections. His eyes assumed the fervid gleam of the fanatic lecturer as he buttoned his shirt.

'Jonathan Wolverton Randall — Wolverton for his mother's uncle, a minor knight from Sussex. He was, however, known by the rather dashing nickname of "Black Jack", something he acquired in the army, probably during the time he was stationed here.' I flopped face down on the bed and affected to snore. Ignoring me, Frank went on with his scholarly exegesis.

'He bought his commission in the mid-thirties – 1730s, that is – and served as a captain of dragoons. According to those old letters Cousin May sent me, he did quite well in the army. Good choice for a second son, you know; his younger brother followed tradition as well by becoming a curate, but I haven't found out much about him yet. Anyway, Jack Randall was highly commended by the Duke of Sandring-ham for his activities before and during the 45 – the second Jacobite Rising, you know,' he amplified for the benefit of the ignorant amongst his audience, namely me. 'You know, Bonnie Prince Charlie and that lot.'

'I'm not entirely sure the Scots realize they lost that one,' I interrupted, sitting up and trying to sub-due my hair. 'I distinctly heard the barman at that pub last night refer to us as Sassenachs.'

'Well, why not?' said Frank equably. 'It only means "Englishman", after all, or at worst, outsider and we're all of that.'

'I know what it means. It was the tone I objected to.'

Frank searched through the chest of drawers for a belt. 'He was just annoyed because I told him the beer was weak. I told him the true Highland brew requires an old boot to be added to the vat, and the final product to be strained through a well-worn undergarment.'

'Ah, that accounts for the amount of the bill.'

'Well, I phrased it a little more tactfully than that, but only because the Gaelic language hasn't got a specific word for drawers.'

I reached for a pair of my own, intrigued. 'Why not? Did the ancient Gaels not wear undergarments?'

Frank leered. 'You've never heard that old song about what a Scotsman wears beneath his kilt?'

'Presumably not gents' knee-length step-ins,' I said dryly. 'Perhaps I'll go out in search of a local kilt-wearer whilst you're cavorting with vicars and ask him.'

'Well, do try not to get arrested, Claire. The dean of St Giles College wouldn't like it at all.'

In the event, there were no kilt-wearers loitering about the town or patronizing the shops. There were a number of other people there, though, mostly housewives of the Mrs Baird type, doing their daily shopping. They were garrulous and gossipy, and their solid, tweedy presences filled the shops with a cosy warmth; a buttress against the cold mist of the morning outdoors.

With as yet no house of my own to keep, I had

little that needed buying – there was little to buy yet, in truth; supplies were still short – but enjoyed myself in browsing among the sparse shelves of the shops.

My gaze lingered on a shop window containing a scattering of household goods – embroidered tea cloths, a set of jug and glasses, a stack of homely pie tins and a set of three vases.

I had never owned a vase in my life. During the war years I had, of course, lived in the nurses' quarters, first at Pembroke Hospital, later at the field station in France. But even before that we had lived nowhere long enough to justify the purchase of such an item. Had I had such a thing, I reflected, Uncle Lamb would have filled it with potsherds long before I could have got near it with a bunch of daisies.

Quentin Lambert Beauchamp. 'Q' to his archaeological students and his friends. 'Dr Beauchamp' to the scholarly circles in which he moved and lectured and had his being. But always Uncle Lamb to me.

My father's only brother, and my only living relative, he had been landed with me, aged five, when my parents were killed in a car crash. Poised for a trip to the Middle East at the time, he had paused in his preparations long enough to make the funeral arrangements, dispose of my parents' estates and enrol me in a proper girls' boarding school. Which I had flatly refused to attend.

Faced with the necessity of prying my chubby fingers off the car's door handle and dragging me by the heels up the steps of the school, Uncle Lamb, who hated personal conflict of any kind, had sighed in exasperation, then finally shrugged and tossed his better judgement out of the window along with my newly purchased round straw boater.

'Ruddy thing,' he muttered, seeing it rolling merrily away in the rear-view mirror as we roared down the drive in high gear. 'Always loathed hats on women, anyway.' He had glanced down at me, fixing me with a fierce glare.

'One thing,' he said, in awful tones. 'You are *not* to play dolls with my Persian grave figurines. Anything else, but not that. Is that clear?'

I had nodded, content. And had gone with him to the Middle East, to South America, to dozens of study sites throughout the world. Had learned to read and write from the drafts of journal articles, to dig latrines and boil water, and to do a number of other things not suitable for a young lady of gentle birth – until I had met the handsome, dark-haired historian who came to consult Uncle Lamb on a point of French philosophy as it related to Egyptian religious practice.

Even after our marriage Frank and I led the nomadic life of junior faculty, divided between continental conferences and temporary flats, until the outbreak of war had sent him to Officer's Training and the Intelligence Unit at MI6, and me to nurse's training. Though we had been married nearly eight years, the new house in Oxford would be our first real home.

Tucking my handbag firmly under my arm, I marched into the shop and bought the vases.

I met Frank at the crossing of the High Street and the Gereside Road and we turned up it together. He raised his eyebrows at my purchases.

'Vases?' He smiled. 'Wonderful. Perhaps now you'll stop putting flowers in my books.'

'They aren't flowers, they're specimens. And it was you who suggested I take up botany. To occupy my mind, now that I've no nursing to do,' I reminded him.

'True.' He nodded good-humouredly. 'But I didn't realize I'd have bits of greenery dropping out into my lap every time I opened a reference. What was that horrible crumbly brown stuff you put in Tuscum and Banks?'

'Comfrey. Good for haemorrhoids.'

'Preparing for my imminent old age, are you? Well, how very thoughtful of you, Claire.'

We had promised to drop in on the Carsons, round the corner. We pushed through the gate, laughing, and Frank stood back to let me go first up the narrow front steps.

Suddenly he caught my arm. 'Look out! You don't want to step in it.'

I lifted my foot gingerly over a large brownish-red stain on the top step.

'How odd,' I said. 'Mrs Carson scrubs the steps down every morning; I've seen her. What do you suppose that can be?'

Frank leaned over the step, sniffing delicately.

'Offhand, I should say that it's blood.'

'Blood!' I took a step back into the entryway. 'Whose?' I glanced nervously into the house. 'Do you suppose the Carsons have had an accident of some kind?' I couldn't imagine our tidy neighbours leaving bloodstains to dry on their doorstep unless some major catastrophe had occurred, and wondered just for a moment whether the parlour might be harbouring a crazed axe-murderer, even now preparing to spring out on us with a spine-chilling shriek.

Frank shook his head. He stood on tiptoe to peer over the hedge into the next garden.

'I shouldn't think so. There's a stain like it on the Collinses' doorstep as well.'

'Really?' I drew closer to Frank, both to see over the hedge and for moral support. The Highlands hardly seemed a likely spot for a mass murderer, but then I doubted such persons used any sort of logical criteria when picking their sites. 'That's rather . . . disagreeable,' I observed. There was no sign of life from the next residence. 'What do you suppose has happened?'

Frank frowned, thinking, then slapped his hand briefly against his trouser leg in inspiration.

'I think I know! Wait here a moment.' He darted out to the gate and set off down the road at a trot, leaving me stranded on the edge of the doorstep.

He was back shortly, beaming with confirmation.

'Yes, that's it, it must be. Every house in the row has had it.'

'Had what? A visit from a homicidal maniac?' I spoke a bit sharply, still nervous at having been abruptly abandoned with nothing but a large blood-stain for company.

Frank laughed. 'No, a ritual sacrifice. Fascinat-ing!' He was down on his hands and knees in the grass, peering interestedly at the stain.

This hardly sounded better than a homicidal maniac. I squatted beside him, wrinkling my nose at the smell. It was early for flies, but a horde of the tiny, voracious Highland midges circled the stain.

'What do you mean, "ritual sacrifice"?' I demanded. 'Mrs Carson's a good church-goer, and so are all the neighbours. This isn't Druid's Hill or anything, you know.'

He stood, brushing grass-ends from his trousers. 'That's all you know, my girl,' he said. 'There's no place on earth with more of the old superstitions and magic mixed into its daily life than the Scottish Highlands. Church or no church, Mrs Carson believes in the Old Folk, and so do all the neighbours.' He pointed at the stain with one neatly polished toe. 'The blood of a black cock,' he explained, looking pleased. 'The houses are new, you see. Pre-fabs.'

I looked at him coldly. 'If you are under the impression that that explains everything, think again. What difference does it make how old the houses are? And where on earth is everybody?'

'Down at the pub, I should expect. Let's go along and see, shall we?' Taking my arm, he steered me out of the gate and we set off down the Gereside Road.

'In the old days,' he explained as we went, 'and not so long ago, either, when a house was built it was customary to kill something and bury it under the foundation, as a propitiation to the local earth spirits. You know, "He shall lay the foundations thereof in his firstborn and in his youngest son shall he set up the gates of it." Old as the hills.'

I shuddered at the quotation. 'In that case, I suppose it's quite modern and enlightened of them to be using chickens instead. You mean, since the houses are fairly new, nothing was buried under them, and the inhabitants are now remedying the omission.'

'Yes, exactly.' Frank seemed pleased with my progress, and patted me on the back. 'According to the minister, many of the local folk thought the war was due in part to people turning away from their roots and omitting to take proper precautions, such as burying a sacrifice under the foundation, that is, or burning fishes' bones on the hearth — except haddocks, of course,' he added, happily distracted. 'You never burn a haddock's bones — did you know? — or you'll never catch another. Always bury the bones of a haddock instead.'

'I'll bear it in mind,' I said. 'Tell me what you do in order never to see another herring, and I'll do it forthwith.'

He shook his head, absorbed in one of his feats of memory, those brief periods of scholastic rapture where he lost touch with the world around him, absorbed completely in conjuring up knowledge from all its sources.

'I don't know about herring,' he said absently. 'For mice, though, you hang bunches of Trembling Jock about — "Trembling Jock i' the hoose, and ye'll ne'er see a moose", you know. Bodies under the foundation, though — that's where a lot of the local ghosts come from. You know Mountgerald, the big house at the end of the High Street? There's a ghost there, a workman on the house who was killed as a sacrifice for the foundation. It was some time in the eighteenth century; that's really fairly recent,' he added thoughtfully.

'The story goes that by order of the house's owner, one wall was built up first, then a stone block was dropped from the top of it on to one of the workmen — presumably a dislikable fellow was chosen for the sacrifice – and he was buried then in the cellar and the rest of the house built up over him. He haunts the cellar where he was killed, except on the anniversary of his death and the four Old Days.'

'Old Days?'

'The ancient feasts,' he explained, still lost in his mental notes. 'Hogmanay, that's New Year's Eve, Midsummer Day, Beltane and All Hallow's, Druids, Beaker Folk, early Picts, everybody kept the sun feasts and the fire feasts, so far as we know. Anyway, ghosts are freed on the holy days, and can wander about at will, to do harm or good as they please.' He rubbed his chin thoughtfully. 'It's getting on for Beltane – the Celtic May Day festival. Best keep an eye out next time you pass the kirkyard.' His eyes twinkled, and I realized the trance had ended.

I laughed. 'Are there a number of famous local ghosts, then?'

He shrugged. 'Don't know. We'll ask Mr Wakefield, shall we, next time we see him?'

We saw Mr Wakefield that evening, in fact. He, along with most of the other inhabitants of the neighbourhood, was in the hotel lounge, having a lemonade in celebration of the houses' new sanctification.

He seemed rather embarrassed at being caught in the act of condoning a paganism, as it were, but brushed it off as merely a local observance with historical colour, like the Wearing of the Green.

'Really rather fascinating, you know,' he confided, and I recognized, with an internal sigh, the song of the scholar, as identifying a sound as the call of a cuckoo. Harking to the sound of a kindred spirit, Frank at once settled down to the mating dance of academe and they were soon neck-deep in archetypes and the parallels between ancient superstitions and modern religions. I snagged a passing waitress and secured a couple of cups of tea.

Knowing from experience how difficult it was to distract Frank's attention from this sort of discussion, I simply picked up his hand, wrapped his fingers about the handle of the cup and left him to his own devices.

I found our landlady, Mrs Baird, on a loveseat near the window, sharing a companionable plate of digestive biscuits with an elderly man whom she introduced to me as Mr Crook.

'This is the man I tell't ye about, Mrs Randall,' she said, eyes bright with the stimulation of company. 'The one as knows about plants of all sorts.

'Mrs Randall's verra much interested in the wee plants,' she confided to her companion, who inclined his head in a combination of politeness and deafness. 'Presses them in books and such.'

'Do ye, indeed?' Mr Crook asked, one tufted white brow raised in interest. 'I've some presses – the real ones, mind – for plants and such. Had them from my nephew, when he came up from university over his holiday. He brought them for me, and I'd not the heart to tell him I never use such things. Hangin's what's wanted for herbs, ye ken, or maybe to be dried on a frame and put in a bit o' gauze bag or a jar, but why ever you'd be after squashing the wee things flat, I've no idea.'

'Well, to look at, maybe,' Mrs Baird interjected kindly. 'Mrs Randall's made some lovely bits out of wood anenome, and violets, same as you could put in a frame and hang on the wall, like.'

'Mmmphm.' Mr Crook's seamed face appeared to be admitting a dubious possibility to this suggestion. 'Weel, if they're of any use to ye, Missus, you can have the presses, and welcome. I didna wish to be throwing them awa', but I must say I've no use for them.'

I assured Mr Crook that I would be delighted to make use of the plant presses, and still more delighted if he would show me where some of the rarer plants in the area could be found. He eyed me sharply for a moment, head to one side like an elderly kestrel, but appeared finally to decide that my interest was genuine, and we fixed it up that I should meet him in the morning for a tour of the local shrubbery. Frank, I knew, meant to spend the morning consulting records in the town hall, and I was pleased to have an excuse not to accompany him. One record was much like another, so far as I was concerned.

Soon after this Frank prised himself away from the minister and we walked home in company with Mrs Baird. I was reluctant to mention the cock's blood we had seen on the doorsteps, myself, but Frank suffered from no such reticence, and questioned her eagerly as to the background of the custom.

'I suppose it's quite old, then?' he asked, swishing a stick along through the roadside weeds. Fat hen and cinquefoil were green in the ditches, and I could see the buds of sweet broom just starting to show.

'Och, aye.' Mrs Baird waddled along at a brisk pace, asking no quarter from our younger limbs. 'Older than anyone knows, Mr Randall. Even back before the days of the giants.'

'Giants?' I asked.

'Aye. Fionn and the Feinn, ye ken.'

'Gaelic folktales,' Frank remarked with interest. 'Heroes, you know. Probably from Norse roots. There's a lot of the Norse influence around here, and all the way up the coast to the West. Some of the place names are Norse, you know, not Gaelic at all.'

I rolled my eyes, sensing another outburst, but Mrs Baird smiled kindly and encouraged him, saying that was true, then; she'd been up to the north, and seen the Two Brothers stone, and that was Norse, wasn't it?

'The Norsemen came down on that coast hundreds of times between AD 500 and 1300 or so,' Frank said, looking dreamily at the horizon, seeing dragon-ships in the windswept cloud. 'Vikings, you know. And they brought a lot of their own myths along. It's a good country for myths. Things seem to take root here.'

This I could believe. Twilight was coming on, and so was a storm. In the eerie light beneath the clouds even the thoroughly modern houses along the road looked as ancient and as sinister as the weathered Pictish stone that stood a hundred feet away, guarding the crossroads it had marked for a thousand years. It seemed a good night to be inside with the shutters fastened.

Rather than staying cosily in Mrs Baird's parlour to be entertained by stereopticon views of Perth, though, Frank chose to keep his appointment for sherry with Mr Bainbridge, a solicitor with an interest in local historical records. Bearing in mind my earlier encounter with Mr Bainbridge, I elected to stay at home.

'Try to come back before the storm breaks,' I said, kissing Frank goodbye. 'And give my regards to Mr Bainbridge.'

'Umm, yes. Yes, of course.' Carefully not meeting my eye, Frank shrugged into his overcoat and left, collecting an umbrella from the stand by the door.

I closed the door after him but left it on the latch so he could get back in. I wandered back towards the parlour, reflecting that Frank would doubtless pretend that he didn't have a wife – a pretence in which Mr Bainbridge would cheerfully join. Not that I could blame him, particularly.

At first, everything had gone quite well on our visit to Mr Bainbridge's home the afternoon before. I had been demure, genteel, intelligent but self-effacing, well groomed and quietly dressed – everything the Perfect Don's Wife should be. Until the tea was served.

I now turned my right hand over, ruefully examining the large blister that ran across the bases of all four fingers. After all, it was not my fault that Mr Bainbridge, a widower, made do with a cheap tin teapot instead of a proper crockery one. Nor that the solicitor, seeking to be polite, had asked me to pour. Nor that the potholder he provided had a worn patch that allowed the red-hot handle of the teapot to come into direct contact with my hand when I picked it up.

No, I decided. Dropping the teapot was a perfectly normal reaction. Dropping it on Mr Bainbridge's carpet was merely an accident of placement; I had to drop it somewhere. It was my exclaiming 'Bloody fucking hell!' in a voice that topped Mr Bainbridge's heartcry that had made Frank glare at me across the scones.

Once he recovered from the shock Mr Bainbridge had been quite gallant, fussing about my hand and ignoring Frank's attempts to excuse my language on grounds that I had been stationed in a field hospital for the better part of two years. 'I'm afraid my wife picked up a number of, er, colourful expressions from the Yanks and such,' Frank offered, with a nervous smile.

'True,' I said, gritting my teeth as I wrapped a water-soaked napkin about my hand. 'Men tend to be very "colourful" when you're picking shrapnel out of them.'

Mr Bainbridge had tactfully tried to distract the conversation on to neutral historical ground by saying that he had always been interested in the variations of what was considered profane speech through the ages. There was 'gorblimey' for example, a recent corruption of the oath 'God blind me'.

'Yes, of course,' said Frank, gratefully accepting the diversion. 'No sugar, thank you, Claire. What about "Gadzooks"? The "Gad" part is quite clear, of course, but the "zook" . . .'

'Well, you know,' the solicitor interjected, 'I've sometimes thought it might be a corruption of an old Scots word, in fact — "yeuk". Means "itch". That would make sense, wouldn't it?'

Frank nodded, letting his unscholarly forelock fall across his forehead. He pushed it back automatically. 'Interesting,' he said, 'the whole evolution of profanity.'

'Yes, and it's still going on,' I said, carefully picking up a lump of sugar with the tongs.

'Oh?' said Mr Bainbridge politely. 'Did you encounter some interesting variations during your, er, war experience?'

'Oh, yes,' I said. 'My favourite was one I picked up from a Yank. Man named Williamson, from New York, I believe. He said it every time I changed his dressing.'

'What was it?'

'"Jesus H. Roosevelt Christ,"' I said, and dropped the sugar lump neatly and deliberately into Frank's cup.

❧

After a peaceful and not unpleasant sit with Mrs Baird, I made my way upstairs to ready myself before Frank came home. I knew his limit with sherry was two glasses, so I expected him back soon.

The wind was rising and the very air of the bed-room was prickly with electricity. I drew the brush through my hair, making the curls snap with static and spring into knots and furious tangles. My hair would have to do without its hundred strokes tonight, I decided. I would settle for brushing my teeth, in this sort of weather. Strands of hair adhered stickily to my cheeks, clinging stubbornly as I tried to smooth them back.

No water in the ewer; Frank had used it, tidying

himself before setting out for his meeting with Mr Bainbridge, and I had not bothered to refill it from the bathroom tap. I picked up the bottle of L'Heure Bleue and poured a generous puddle into the palm of my hand. Rubbing my hands briskly together before the scent could evaporate, I smoothed them rapidly through my hair. I poured another dollop on to my hairbrush and swept the curls back behind my ears with it.

Well. That was rather better, I thought, turning my head from side to side to examine the results in the speckled looking glass. The moisture had dissipated the static electricity in my hair so that it floated in heavy, shining waves about my face. And the evaporating alcohol had left behind a very pleasant scent. Frank would like that, I thought. L'Heure Bleue was his favourite.

There was a sudden flash close at hand, with the crash of thunder following hard on its heels, and all the lights went out. Cursing under my breath, I groped in the drawers.

Somewhere I had seen candles and matches; power failure was so frequent an occurrence in the Highlands that candles were a necessary furnishing for all inn and hotel rooms. I had seen them even in the Royal Edinburgh, where they were scented with honeysuckle and elegantly presented in frosted glass holders with shimmering pendants.

Mrs Baird's candles were far more utilitarian — plain white household candles — but there were a lot of them, and three boxes of matches as well. I was not inclined to be fussy over style at a time like this.

I fitted a candle to the blue ceramic holder on the dressing table by the light of the next flash, then moved about the room, lighting others, till the whole room was filled with a soft, wavering radiance. Very romantic, I thought, and with some presence of mind I pressed down the light switch so that a sudden return of power shouldn't ruin the mood at some inopportune moment.

The candles had burned no more than half an inch when the door opened and Frank blew in. Literally, for the draught that followed him up the stairs extinguished three of the candles.

The door closed behind him with a bang that blew out two more, and he peered into the sudden gloom, pushing a hand through his dishevelled hair. I got up and relit the candles, making mild remarks about his abrupt methods of entering rooms. It was only when I had finished and turned to ask him whether he'd like a drink that I saw he was looking rather white and unsettled.

'What's the matter?' I said. 'Seen a ghost?'

'Well, you know,' he said slowly, 'I'm not at all sure that I haven't.' Absentmindedly he picked up my hairbrush and raised it to tidy his hair. When a sudden whiff of L'Heure Bleue reached his nostrils, he wrinkled his nose and set it down again, settling for the attentions of his pocket comb instead.

I glanced through the window, where the lime trees were lashing to and fro like flails. It occurred to me that we ought perhaps to close our shutters, though the carry-on outside was rather exciting to watch.

'Bit blustery for a ghost, I'd think,' I said. 'Don't they like quiet, misty evenings in graveyards?'

Frank laughed a bit sheepishly. 'Well, I daresay it's only Bainbridge's stories, plus a bit more of his sherry than I really meant to have. Nothing at all, probably.'

Now I was curious. 'What exactly did you see?' I asked, settling myself on the dressing-table seat. I motioned to the whisky bottle with a half-lifted brow, and Frank went at once to pour a couple of drinks.

'Well, only a man, really,' he began, measuring out a tot for himself and two for me. 'Standing down in the road outside.'

'What, outside this house?' I laughed. 'Must have been a ghost, then; I can't imagine any living person standing about on a night like this.'

Frank tilted the ewer over his glass, then looked accusingly at me when no water came out.

'Don't look at me,' I said. 'You used up all the water. I don't mind it neat, though.' I took a sip in illustration.

Frank looked as though he were tempted to nip down to the bathroom for water, but abandoned the idea and went on with his story, sipping cautiously as though his glass contained vitriol rather than the most expensive product of the local illicit stills.

'Yes, he was down at the edge of the garden on this side, standing by the hedge. I thought' — he hesitated, looking down into his glass — 'I rather thought he was looking up at your window.'

'My window? How extraordinary!' I couldn't repress a mild shiver, and went across to fasten the shutters, though it seemed a bit late for that. Frank followed me across the room, still talking.

'Yes, I could see you myself from below. You were brushing your hair and cursing a bit because it was standing on end.'

'In that case, the fellow was probably enjoying a good laugh,' I said tartly. Frank shook his head, though he smiled and smoothed his hands over my hair.

'No, he wasn't laughing. In fact, he seemed terribly unhappy about something. Not that I could see his face well; just something about the way he stood. I came up behind him, and when he didn't move, I asked politely if I could help him with something. He acted at first as though he didn't hear me, and I thought perhaps he didn't, over the noise of the wind, so I repeated myself, and I reached out to tap his shoulder, to get his attention, you know. But before I could touch him he whirled suddenly round and pushed past me and walked off down the road.'

'Sounds a bit rude, but not very ghostly,' I observed, draining my glass. 'What did he look like?'

'Big chap,' said Frank, frowning in recollection. 'And a Scot, in complete Highland rig-out, complete to sporran and the most beautiful running-stag brooch on his plaid. I wanted to ask where he'd got it from, but he was off before I could.'

I went to the chest of drawers and poured another drink. 'Well, not so unusual an appearance for these parts, surely? I've seen men dressed like that in the village now and then.'

'Nooo . . .' Frank sounded doubtful. 'No, it wasn't his dress that was odd. But when he pushed past me I could swear he was close enough that I should have felt him brush my sleeve — but I didn't. And I was intrigued enough to turn round and watch him as he walked away. He walked down the Gereside Road, but when he'd almost reached the corner, he . . . disappeared. That's when I began to feel a bit cold down the backbone.'

'Perhaps your attention was distracted for a second and he just stepped aside into the shadows,' I suggested. 'There are a lot of trees down near that corner.'

'I could swear I didn't take my eyes off him for a

moment,' muttered Frank. He looked up suddenly. 'I know! I remember now why I thought he was so odd, though I didn't realize it at the time.'

'What?' I was getting a bit tired of the ghost, and wanted to go on to more interesting matters, such as bed.

'The wind was cutting up like billy-o, but his drapes – his kilt and his plaid, you know – they didn't move at all, except to the stir of his walking.'

We stared at each other. 'Well,' I said finally, 'that is a bit spooky.'

Frank shrugged and smiled suddenly, dismissing it. 'At least I'll have something to tell the minister next time I see him. Perhaps it's a well-known local ghost, and he can give me its gory history.' He glanced at his watch. 'But now I'd say it's bedtime.'

'So it is,' I murmured.

I watched him in the mirror as he removed his shirt and reached for a hanger. Suddenly he paused in mid-button.

'Did you have many Scots in your charge, Claire?' he asked abruptly. 'At the field hospital, or at Pembroke?'

'Of course,' I replied, somewhat puzzled. 'There were quite a few of the Seaforths and Camerons through the field hospital at Amiens, and then a bit later, after Caen, we had a lot of the Gordons. Nice chaps, most of them. Very stoic about things generally, but terrible cowards about injections.' I smiled, remembering one in particular.

'We had one – rather a crusty old thing really, a piper from the Third Seaforths – who couldn't stand being stuck, especially not in the hip. He'd go for hours in the most awful discomfort before he'd let anyone near him with a needle, and even then he'd try to get us to give him the injection in the arm, though it's meant to be intramuscular.' I laughed at the memory of Corporal Chisholm. 'He told me, "If I'm goin' to lie on my face wi' my buttocks bared, I want the lass *under* me, not behind me wi' a hatpin!"'

Frank smiled, but looked a trifle uneasy as he often did about my less delicate war stories. 'Don't worry,' I assured him, seeing the look, 'I won't tell that one at tea in the Senior Common Room.'

The smile lightened and he came forward to stand behind me as I sat at the dressing table. He pressed a kiss on the top of my head.

'Don't worry,' he said. 'The Senior Common Room will love you, no matter what stories you tell. Mmmm. Your hair smells wonderful.'

'Do you like it then?' His hands slid forward over my shoulders in answer, cupping my breasts in the thin nightdress. I could see his head above mine in the mirror, his chin resting on top of my head.

'I like everything about you,' he said huskily. 'You look wonderful by candlelight, you know. Your eyes are like sherry in crystal, and your skin glows like ivory. A candlelight witch, you are. Perhaps I should disconnect the lamps permanently.'

'Make it hard to read in bed,' I said, my heart beginning to speed up.

'I could think of better things to do in bed,' he murmured.

'Could you, indeed?' I said, rising and turning to put my arms about his neck. 'Like what?'

Some time later, cuddled close behind bolted shutters, I lifted my head from his shoulder and said, 'Why did you ask me that earlier? About whether I'd had anything to do with any Scots, I mean – you must know I had, there are all sorts of men through those hospitals.'

He stirred and ran a hand softly down my back.

'Mmm. Oh, nothing, really. Just, when I saw that chap outside, it occurred to me he might be' – he hesitated, tightening his hold a bit – 'er, you know, that he might have been someone you'd nursed, perhaps . . . maybe heard you were staying here, and came along to see . . . something like that.'

'In that case,' I said practically, 'why wouldn't he come in and ask to see me?'

'Well,' Frank's voice was very casual, 'maybe he didn't want particularly to run into me.'

I pushed up on to one elbow, staring at him. We had left one candle burning, and I could see him well enough. He had turned his head and was looking oh-so-casually off towards the chromolithograph of Bonnie Prince Charlie with which Mrs Baird had seen fit to decorate our wall.

I grabbed his chin and turned his head to face me. He widened his eyes in simulated surprise.

'Are you implying,' I demanded, 'that the man you saw outside was some sort of, of . . .' I hesitated, looking for the proper word.

'Liaison?' he suggested helpfully.

'Romantic interest of mine?' I finished.

'No, no, certainly not,' he said unconvincingly. He took my hands away from his face and tried to kiss me, but now it was my turn for head-turning. He settled for pressing me back down to lie beside him.

'It's only . . .' he began. 'Well, you know, Claire, it *was* six years. And we saw each other only three times, and only just for the day that last time. It wouldn't be unusual if . . . I mean, everyone knows doctors and nurses are under tremendous stress during emergencies, and . . . well, I . . . it's just that . . . well, I'd understand, you know, if anything, er, of a spontaneous nature . . .'

I interrupted this rambling by jerking free and exploding out of bed.

'Do you think I've been unfaithful to you?' I demanded. 'Do you? Because if so, you can leave this room this instant. Leave the house altogether! How dare you imply such a thing?' I was seething, and Frank, sitting up, reached out to try to soothe me.

'Don't you touch me!' I snapped. 'Just tell me – *do* you think, on the evidence of a strange man happening to glance up at my window, that I've had some flaming affair with one of my patients?'

Frank got out of bed and wrapped his arms around me. I stayed stiff as Lot's wife, but he persisted, caressing my hair and rubbing my shoulders in the way he knew I liked.

'No, I don't think any such thing,' he said firmly. He pulled me closer and I relaxed slightly, though not enough to put my arms around him.

After a long time he murmured into my hair, 'No, I know you'd never do such a thing. I only meant to say that even if you ever did . . . Claire, it would make no difference to me. I love you so. Nothing you ever did could stop my loving you.' He took my face between his hands – only four inches taller than I, he could look directly into my eyes without trouble – and said softly, 'Forgive me?' His breath, barely scented with the tang of whisky, was warm on my face, and his lips, full and inviting, were disturbingly close.

Another rumble of thunder heralded the sudden breaking of the storm, and a thundering rain smashed down on the slates of the roof.

I slowly put my arms around his waist.

' "The quality of mercy is not strained," ' I quoted. ' "It droppeth as the gentle rain from heaven . . . " '

Frank laughed and looked upwards; the overlapping stains on the ceiling boded ill for the prospects of our sleeping dry all night.

'If that's a sample of your mercy,' he said, 'I'd hate to see your vengeance.' The thunder went off like a mortar attack, as though in answer to his words, and we both laughed, at ease again.

It was only later, listening to his regular deep breathing beside me, that I began to wonder. As I had said, there was no evidence whatsoever to imply unfaithfulness on my part. *My* part. But six years, as he'd said, was a long time.

2

Standing Stones

Mr Crook called for me, as arranged, promptly at seven the next morning.

'So as we'll catch the dew on the buttercups, eh, lass?' he said, twinkling with elderly gallantry. He had brought a motorcycle of his own approximate vintage, on which to transport us into the country-side. The plant presses were tidily strapped to the sides of this enormous machine, like fenders on a tugboat. It was a leisurely ramble through the quiet countryside, made all the more quiet by contrast with the thunderous roar of Mr Crook's cycle, suddenly throttled into silence. The old man did indeed know a lot about the local plants, I discovered. Not only where they were to be found but their medicinal uses, and how to prepare them. I wished I had brought a notebook to get it all down, but listened intently to the cracked old voice and did my best to commit the information to memory as I stowed our specimens in the heavy plant presses.

We stopped for a packed luncheon near the base of a curious flat-topped hill. Green as most of its neighbours, with the same rocky juts and crags, it had something different: a well-worn path leading up one side and disappearing abruptly behind an outcrop.

'What's up there?' I asked, gesturing with a cheese and pickle sandwich. 'It seems a difficult place for picnicking.'

'Ah.' Mr Crook glanced at the hill. 'That's Craigh na Dun, lass. I'd meant to show ye after our meal.'

'Really? Is there something special about it?'

'Oh, aye,' he answered, but refused to elaborate further, merely saying that I'd see when I saw.

I had some fears about his ability to climb such a steep path, but these evaporated as I found myself panting in his wake. At last Mr Crook extended a gnarled hand and pulled me up over the rim of the hill.

'There it is.' He waved a hand with a sort of proprietorial gesture.

'Why, it's a henge!' I said, delighted. 'A miniature henge!'

Because of the war it had been several years since I had last visited Salisbury Plain, but Frank and I had seen Stonehenge soon after we were married. Like the other tourists wandering awed among the huge standing stones we had gaped at the Altar Stone ('where ancient Druid priests performed their dreadful human sacrifices,' announced our sonorous cockney guide).

Out of the same passion for exactness that made Frank adjust his ties on the hanger so that the ends hung precisely so, we had even trekked around the circumference of the circle, pacing off the distance between the Z holes and the Y holes, and counting the lintels over the Sarsen Circle, the outermost ring of monstrous uprights.

Three hours later, we knew how many Y and Z holes there were (fifty-nine, if you care; I didn't), but had no more clue to the purpose of the structure than had the dozens of amateur and professional archaeologists who had crawled over the site for the last five hundred years.

No lack of opinions, of course. Life among academics had taught me that a well-expressed opinion is usually better than a badly expressed fact, so far as professional advancement goes.

A temple. A burial ground. An astronomical observatory. A place of execution (hence the aptly named Slaughter Stone that lies to one side, half sunk in its own pit). An open-air market. I liked this last suggestion, visualizing Megalithic housewives strolling between the lintels, baskets on their arms, critically judging the glaze on the latest shipment of red-clay beakers and listening sceptically to the claims of stone-age bakers and vendors of deer-bone shovels and amber beads.

The only thing I could see against that hypothesis was the presence of bodies under the Altar Stone and cremated remains in the Z holes. Unless these were the hapless remains of merchants accused of short-weighting the customers, it seemed a bit insanitary to be burying people in the marketplace.

There were no signs of burial in the miniature henge atop this hill. By miniature I mean only that the circle of standing stones was smaller than Stonehenge; each stone was still twice my own height, and massive in proportion.

I had heard from another guide at Stonehenge that these stone circles occur all over Britain and Europe — some in better repair than others, some differing slightly in orientation or form, all of purpose and origin unknown.

Mr Crook stood smiling benignly as I prowled among the stones, pausing now and then to touch one gently, as though my touch could make an impression on the monumental boulders.

Some of the standing stones were brindled, striped with dim colours. Others were speckled with flakes of mica that caught the sun with a cheerful shimmer. All of them were remarkably different from the clumps of native stone that thrust out of the bracken all around. Whoever built the stone circles, and for whatever purpose, thought it important enough to have quarried, shaped and transported special stone blocks for the erection of their testimonial. Shaped – how? Transported – how, and from what unimaginable distance?

'My husband would be fascinated,' I told Mr Crook, stopping to thank him for showing me the place and the plants. 'I'll bring him up to see it later.' The gnarled old man gallantly offered me an arm at the top of the trail. I took it, deciding after one look down the precipitous decline that in spite of his age he was probably steadier on his pins than I was.

I swung down the road that afternoon towards the town, to fetch Frank from the manse. I happily breathed in that heady Highland mix of peat and evergreen, spiced here and there with woodsmoke and the tang of fried herring. Those houses near the road were nice. Some were newly painted and even the manse which must be at least a hundred years old, sported fresh maroon trim around its sagging window frames.

The minister's housekeeper answered the door, a tall, stringy woman with three strands of artificial pearls round her neck. Hearing who I was, she welcomed me in and towed me down a long, narrow, dark hallway, lined with sepia engravings of people who may have been famous personages of their time, or cherished relatives of the present minister, but might as well have been the Royal Family, for all I could see of their features in the gloom.

By contrast the minister's study was blinding with light from the enormous windows that ran nearly from the ceiling to floor in one wall. An easel near the fireplace, bearing a half-finished oil of black cliffs against the evening sky, showed the reason for the windows, which must have been added long after the house was built.

Frank and a short, tubby man with a dog collar were cosily poring over a mass of tattered paper on the desk by the far wall. Frank barely looked up in greeting, but the minister politely left off his explanations and hurried over to clasp my hand, his round face beaming with sociable delight.

'Mrs Randall!' he said, pumping my hand heartily. 'How nice to see you again. And you've come just in time to hear the news!'

'News?' Casting an eye on the grubbiness and typeface of the papers on the desk, I calculated the date of the news in question as being around 1750. Not precisely stop-the-presses, then.

'Yes, indeed. We've been tracing your husband's

ancestor, Jack Randall, through the army dispatches of the period.' The minister leaned close, speaking out of the side of his mouth like a gangster in an American film. 'I've, er, "borrowed" the original dispatches from the local Historical Society files. You'll be careful not to tell anyone?'

Amused, I agreed that I would not reveal his deadly secret, and looked about for a comfortable chair in which to receive the latest revelations from the eighteenth century. The wing chair nearest the windows looked suitable, but as I reached to turn it towards the desk I discovered that it was already occupied. The inhabitant, a small boy with a shock of glossy black hair, was curled up in the depths of the chair, sound asleep.

'Roger!' The minister, coming to assist me, was as surprised as I. The boy, startled out of sleep, shot bolt upright, wide eyes the colour of moss.

'Now what are you up to in here, you young scamp?' the minister scolded affectionately. 'Oh, fell asleep reading the comic papers again?' He scooped up the pages and handed them to the lad. 'Run along now, Roger, I have business with the Randalls. Oh, wait, I've forgotten to introduce you – Mrs Randall, this is my son, Roger.'

I was a bit surprised. If ever I'd seen a confirmed bachelor I would have thought the Reverend Mr Wakefield was it. Still, I took the politely proffered paw and shook it warmly, resisting the urge to wipe a certain residual stickiness on my skirt.

The Reverend Mr Wakefield looked fondly after the boy as he went off towards the kitchen.

'My niece's son, really,' he confided. 'Father shot down over the Channel, and mother killed in the Blitz, though, so I've taken him.'

'How kind of you,' I murmured, thinking of Uncle Lamb. He, too, had died in the Blitz, on his way to the British Museum, where he had been lecturing. Knowing him, I thought his main feeling would have been gratification that the bomb had not hit the museum.

'Not at all, not at all.' The minister flapped a hand in embarrassment. 'Nice to have a bit of young life about the house. Now, do have a seat.'

Frank began talking even before I had set my handbag down. 'The most amazing luck, Claire,' he enthused, thumbing through the dog-eared pile. 'The minister's located a whole series of military dispatches that mention Jonathan Randall.'

'Well, a good deal of the prominence seems to have been Captain Randall's own doing,' the minister observed, taking some of the papers from Frank. 'He was in command of the garrison at Fort William for four years or so, but he seems to have spent quite a bit of his time harassing the Scottish countryside on behalf of the Crown. This lot' – he gingerly separated a stack of papers and laid them on the desk – 'is reports of complaints lodged against the Captain by various families and estate holders, claiming everything from interference with their maidservants by the soldiers of the garrison to outright theft of horses, not to mention assorted instances of "insult", unspecified.'

I was amused. 'So you have the proverbial horse thief in your family tree?' I said to Frank.

He shrugged, unperturbed. 'He was what he was, and there's nothing I can do about it. I only want to find out. The complaints aren't all that odd, for that particular period; the English in general, and the army in particular, were rather notably unpopular throughout the Highlands. No, what's odd is that nothing ever seems to have come of the complaints, even the serious ones.'

The minister, unable to keep still for long, broke in. 'That's right. Not that officers then were held to anything like modern standards; they could do very much as they liked in minor matters. But this is odd. It's not that the complaints are investigated and dismissed; they're just never mentioned again. You know what I suspect, Randall? Your ancestor must have had a patron. Someone who could protect him from the censure of his superiors.'

Frank scratched his head, squinting at the dispatches. 'You could be right. Had to have been someone quite powerful, though. High up in the army hierarchy, perhaps, or another member of the nobility outside the army.'

'Yes, or possibly —' The minister was interrupted in his theories by the entrance of Mrs Graham, the housekeeper.

'I've brought ye a wee bit of refreshment, gentle-men,' she announced, setting the tea tray firmly in the centre of the desk, from which the minister res-cued his precious dispatches in the nick of time. She looked me over with a shrewd eye, assessing the twitching limbs and faint glaze over the eyeballs.

'I've brought but the two cups, for I thought per-haps Mrs Randall would care to join me in the kitchen. I've a bit of —' I didn't wait for the conclu-sion of her invitation, but leapt to my feet with alacrity. I could hear the theories breaking out again behind me as we pushed through the swinging door that led to the manse's kitchen.

The tea was hot and fragrant, with bits of leaf swirling through the liquid.

'Mmm,' I said, setting the cup down. 'It's been a long time since I tasted Earl Grey.'

Mrs Graham nodded, beaming at my pleasure in her refreshments. She had clearly gone to some trouble, laying out handmade lace doilies beneath the eggshell cups and providing real butter and jam with the scones.

'Aye, I save it special for the readings. Better than the Indian stuff, ye know.'

'Oh, you read tea leaves?' I asked, mildly amused. Nothing could be further from the popular conception of the gypsy fortune-teller than Mrs Graham, with her short, iron-grey perm and triple-stranded pearl choker. A swallow of tea ran visibly down the long, stringy neck and disappeared beneath the gleaming beads.

'Why, certainly I do, my dear. Just as my grandmother taught me, and her grandmother before her. Drink up your cup, and I'll see what you have there.'

She was silent for a long time, once in a while tilting the cup to catch the light, or rolling it slowly between lean palms to get a different angle.

She set the cup down carefully, as though afraid it might blow up in her face. The grooves on either side of her mouth had deepened, and her brows pressed together in what looked like puzzlement.

'Well,' she said finally. 'That's one of the stranger cups I've seen.'

'Oh?' I was still amused, but beginning to be curious. 'Am I going to meet a tall dark stranger, or journey across the sea?'

'Could be.' Mrs Graham had caught my ironic tone, and echoed it, smiling slightly. 'And could not. That's what's odd about your cup, my dear. Everything in it's contradictory. There's the curved leaf for a journey, but it's crossed by the broken one that means staying put. And strangers there are, to be sure, several of them. And one of them's your husband, if I read the leaves aright.'

My amusement dissipated somewhat. After six years apart, my husband *was* still something of a stranger. Though I failed to see how a tea leaf could know it.

Mrs Graham's brow was still furrowed. 'Let me see your hand, child,' she said.

The hand holding mine was bony, but surprisingly warm. A scent of lavender water emanated from the neat parting of the grizzled head bent over my palm. She stared into my hand for quite a long time, now and then tracing one of the lines with a finger as though following a map whose roads all petered out in sandy washes and deserted wastes.

'Well, what is it?' I asked, trying to maintain a light air. 'Or is my fate too horrible to be revealed?'

Mrs Graham raised quizzical eyes and looked thoughtfully at my face, but retained her hold on my hand. She shook her head, pursing her lips.

'Oh no, my dear. It's not your fate is in your hand. Only the seed of it.' The birdlike head cocked to one side, considering. 'The lines in your hand change, ye know. At another point in your life, they may be quite different than they are now.'

'I didn't know that. I thought you were born with

them, and that was that.' I was repressing an urge to jerk my hand away. 'What's the point of palm reading, then?' I didn't wish to sound rude, but I found this scrutiny a bit unsettling, especially following on the heels of that tea leaf reading. Mrs Graham smiled unexpectedly and folded my fingers closed over my palm.

'Why, the lines of your palm show what ye are, dear. That's why they change – or should. They don't, in some people; those unlucky enough never to change in themselves, but there are few like that.' She gave my folded hand a squeeze and patted it. 'I doubt that you're one of those. Your hand shows quite a lot of change already, for one so young. That would likely be the war, of course,' she said, as though to herself.

I was curious again, and opened my palm voluntarily.

'What am I, then, according to my hand?'

Mrs Graham frowned, but did not pick up my hand again.

'I canna just say. It's odd, for most hands have a likeness to them. Mind, I'd no just say that it's "see one, you've seen them all", but it's often like that – there are patterns, you know.' She smiled suddenly, an oddly engaging grin, displaying very white and patently false teeth.

'That's how a fortune-teller works, you know. I do it for the church fête every year – or did, before the war; suppose I'll do it again now. But a girl comes into the tent — and there am I, done up in a turban with a peacock feather borrowed from Mr Donaldson, and "robes of oriental splendour" — that's the minister's dressing gown, all over peacocks it is and yellow as the sun — anyway, I look her over while I pretend to be watching her hand, and I see she's got her blouse cut down to her breakfast, cheap scent, and earrings down to her shoulders. I needn't have a crystal ball to be tellin' her she'll have a child before the next year's fête.' Mrs Graham paused, grey eyes alight with mischief. 'Though if the hand you're holding is bare, it's tactful to predict first that she'll marry soon.'

I laughed, and so did she. 'So you don't look at their hands at all, then?' I asked. 'Except to check for rings?'

She looked surprised. 'Oh, of course you do. It's just that you know ahead of time what you'll see. Generally.' She nodded at my open hand. 'But that is not a pattern I've seen before. The large thumb, now' — she did lean forward then and touch it lightly — 'that wouldn't change much. Means you're strong-minded and have a will not easily crossed.' She twinkled at me. 'Reckon your husband could have told ye that. Likewise about that one.' She pointed to the fleshy mound at the base of the thumb.

'What is it?'

'The Mount of Venus, it's called.' She pursed her

thin lips primly together, though the corners turned irrepressibly up. 'In a man, ye'd say it means he likes the lasses. For a woman, 'tis a bit different. To be polite about it, I'll make a bit of a prediction for you, and say your husband isna like to stray far from your bed.' She gave a surprisingly deep and bawdy chuckle, and I blushed slightly.

The elderly housekeeper pored over my hand again, stabbing a pointed forefinger here and there to mark her words.

'Now, there, a well-marked lifeline; you're in good health and likely to stay so. The lifeline's interrupted, meaning your life's changed markedly — well, that's true of us all, is it not? But yours is more chopped-up, like, than I usually see; all bits and pieces. And your marriage-line, now' — she shook her head again — 'it's divided; that's not unusual, means two marriages . . .'

My reaction was slight and immediately suppressed, but she caught the flicker and looked up at once. I thought she probably was quite a shrewd fortune-teller, at that. The grey head shook reassuringly at me.

'No, no, lass. It doesna mean anything's like to happen to your good man. It's only that if it did' — she emphasized the 'if' with a slight squeeze of my hand — 'you'd not be one to pine away and waste the rest of your life in mourning. What it means is, you're one of those can love again if your first love's lost.'

She squinted nearsightedly at my palm, running a short, ridged nail gently down the deep marriage line. 'But most divided lines are broken — yours is forked.' She looked up with a roguish smile. 'Sure you're not a bigamist, on the quiet, like?'

I shook my head, laughing. 'No. When would I have the time?' Then I turned my hand, showing the outer edge.

'I've heard that small marks on the side of the hand indicate how many children you'll have?' My tone was casual, I hoped. The edge of my palm was disappointingly smooth.

Mrs Graham flicked a scornful hand at this idea.

'Pah! After ye've had a bairn or two, ye might show lines there. More like you'd have them on your face. Proves nothing at all beforehand.'

'Oh, it doesn't?' I was foolishly relieved to hear this. I was going to ask whether the deep lines across the base of my wrist meant anything (a potential for suicide?) but we were interrupted at that point by the Reverend Mr Wakefield coming into the kitchen bearing the empty teacups. He set them on the draining board and began a loud and clumsy fumbling through the cupboard, obviously in hopes of provoking help.

Mrs Graham sprang to her feet to defend the sanctity of her kitchen and pushing the Reverend adroitly to one side, set about assembling sherry and biscuits on a tray for the study. He drew me to one side, safely out of the way.

'Why don't you come to the study and have sherry with me and your husband, Mrs Randall? We've made really the most gratifying discovery.'

I could see that in spite of outward composure he was bursting with the glee of whatever they had found, like a small boy with a toad in his pocket. Plainly I was going to have to go and read Captain Jonathan Randall's laundry bill, his receipt for boot repairs or some document of similar fascination.

Frank was so absorbed in the tattered documents that he scarcely looked up when I entered the study. He reluctantly surrendered them to the minister's podgy hands, and came round to stand behind him and peer over his shoulder, as though he could not bear to let the papers out of his sight for a moment.

'Yes?' I said politely, fingering the dirty bits of paper. 'Ummm, yes, very interesting.' In fact, the spidery handwriting was so faded and so ornate that it hardly seemed worth the trouble of deciphering it. One sheet, better preserved than the rest, had some sort of crest at the top.

'The Duke of . . . Sandringham, is it?' I asked, peering at the crest with its faded leopard couchant, and the printing below, more legible than the handwriting.

'Yes, indeed,' the minister said, beaming even more. 'An extinct title, now, you know.'

I didn't, but nodded intelligently, being no stranger to historians in the manic grip of discovery. It was seldom necessary to do more than nod periodically, saying 'Oh, really?' or 'How perfectly fascinating!' at appropriate intervals.

After a certain amount of deferring back and forth between Frank and the minister, the latter won the honour of telling me about their discovery. Evidently, all this rubbish made it appear that Frank's ancestor, the notorious Black Jack Randall, had not been merely a gallant soldier for the Crown, but a trusted – and secret – agent of the Duke of Sandringham.

'Almost an agent provocateur, wouldn't you say, Dr Randall?' The minister graciously handed the ball back to Frank, who seized it and ran.

'Yes, indeed. The language is very guarded, of course . . .' He turned the pages gently with a scrubbed forefinger.

'Oh, really?' I said.

'But it seems from this that Jonathan Randall was entrusted with the job of stirring up Jacobite sentiments, if any existed, among the prominent Scottish families in his area. The point being to smoke out any baronets and clan chieftains who might be harbouring secret sympathies in that direction. But that's odd. Wasn't Sandringham a suspected Jacobite himself?' Frank turned to the minister, a frown of inquiry on his face. The minister's smooth, bald head creased in an identical frown.

'Why, yes, I believe you're right. But wait, let's check in Cameron' – he made a dive for the book-shelf, crammed with calf-bound volumes – 'he's sure to mention Sandringham.'

'How perfectly fascinating,' I murmured, allowing my attention to wander to the huge notice board that filled one wall of the study from floor to ceiling.

It was covered with an amazing assortment of things; mostly papers of one sort or another, gas bills, correspondence, notices about the General Assembly, loose pages of novels, notes in the minister's own hand, but also small items like keys, bottle caps and what appeared to be small car parts, attached with tacks and string.

I browsed idly through the miscellanea, keeping half an ear tuned to the argument going on behind me (the Duke of Sandringham probably *was* a Jaco-bite, they decided). My attention was caught by a genealogical chart, tacked up with special care in a spot by itself, using four tacks, one to a corner. The top of the chart included names dated in the early seventeenth century. But it was the name at the bot-tom of the chart that had caught my eye: 'Roger W. (MacKenzie) Wakefield', it read.

'Excuse me,' I said, interrupting a final sputter of dispute as to whether the leopard in the Duke's crest had a lily in its paw, or was it meant to be a crocus? 'Is this your son's chart?'

'Eh? Oh, why yes, yes it is.' Distracted, the minister hurried over, beaming once more. He detached the chart tenderly from the board and laid it on the table in front of me.

'I didn't want him to forget his own family, you see,' he explained. 'It's quite an old lineage, back to the sixteen hundreds.' His stubby forefinger traced the line of descent almost reverently.

'I gave him my own name because it seemed more suitable, as he lives here, but I didn't want him to forget where he came from.' He made an apologetic grimace. 'I'm afraid my own family is nothing to boast of, genealogically. Ministers and curates, with the occasional bookseller thrown in for variety, and only traceable back to 1762 or so. Rather poor record-keeping, you know,' he said, wagging his head remorsefully over the lethargy of his ancestors.

It was growing late by the time we finally left the manse, with the minister promising to take the letters to town for copying first thing in the morning. Frank babbled happily of spies and Jacobites most of the way back to Mrs Baird's. Finally, though, he noticed my quietness.

'What is it, love?' he asked, taking my arm solicitously. 'Not feeling well?' This was asked with a mingled tone of concern and hope.

'No, I'm quite well. I was only thinking . . .' I hesitated, because we had discussed this matter before. 'I was thinking about Roger.'

'Roger?'

I gave a sigh of impatience. 'Really, Frank! You can be so . . . oblivious! Roger, the Reverend Mr Wakefield's son.'

'Oh. Yes, of course,' he said vaguely. 'Charming child. What about him?'

'Well . . . only that there are a lot of children like that. Orphaned, you know.'

He gave me a sharp look and shook his head.

'No, Claire. Really, I'd like to, but I've told you how I feel about adoption. It's just . . . I couldn't feel properly towards a child who's not . . . well, not of my blood. No doubt that's ridiculous and selfish of me, but there it is. Maybe I'll change my mind in time, but now . . .' We walked a few steps in a barbed silence. Suddenly he stopped and turned to me, gripping my hands.

'Claire,' he said huskily, 'I want *our* child. You're the most important thing in the world to me. I want you to be happy, above all else, but I want . . . well, I want to keep you to myself. I'm afraid a child from outside, one we had no real relationship with, would seem an intruder, and I'd resent it. But to be able to give you a child, see it grow in you . . . then I'd feel as though it were more an . . . extension of you, perhaps.

And me. A real part of the family.' His eyes were wide, pleading.

'Yes, all right. I understand.' I was willing to abandon the topic – for now. I turned to go on walking but he reached out and took me in his arms.

'Claire. I love you.' The tenderness in his voice was overwhelming, and I leaned my head against his jacket, feeling his warmth and the strength of his arms around me.

'I love you too.' We stood locked together for a moment, swaying slightly in the wind that swept down the road. Suddenly Frank drew back a bit, smiling down at me.

'Besides,' he said softly, smoothing the windblown hair back from my face, 'we haven't given up yet, have we?'

I smiled back. 'No.'

He took my hand, tucking it snugly beneath his elbow, and we turned towards our lodgings.

'Game for another try?'

'Yes. Why not?' We strolled, hand in hand, back towards the Gereside Road. It was the sight of the Clach Mhor, the Pictish stone that stands at the corner of the road there, that made me remember things ancient.

'I forgot!' I exclaimed. 'I have something exciting to show you.' Frank looked down at me and pulled me closer. He squeezed my hand.

'So have I,' he said, grinning. 'You can show me yours tomorrow.'

When tomorrow came, though, we had other things to do. I had forgotten that we had planned a day trip to the Great Glen and Loch Ness. It was after nine when we arrived at Lochend and the guide Frank had called for was awaiting us on the edge of the loch with a small sailing skiff.

'An' it suits ye, sir, I thought we'd take a wee sail down the loch-side to Urquhart Castle. Perhaps we'll have a wee bit and sup there, before goin' on.' The guide, a dour-looking little man in weather-beaten cotton shirt and twill trousers, stowed the picnic hamper tidily beneath the seat and offered me a calloused hand down into the well of the boat.

It was a beautiful day, with the burgeoning greenery of the steep banks blurring in the ruffled surface of the loch. Our guide, despite his dour appearance, was knowledgeable and talkative, pointing out the landmarks that rimmed the long, narrow loch.

'Yonder, that's Urquhart Castle.' He pointed to a picturesque stone ruin above the loch. 'Or what's left of it. 'Twas cursed by the witches of the Glen, and saw one unhappiness after another.'

He told us the story of Mary Grant, daughter of

the laird of Urquhart Castle, and her lover, Donald Donn, poet son of MacDonald of Bohuntin. Forbidden to meet because of her father's objection to the latter's habits of lifting any cattle he came across (an old and honourable Highland profession, the guide assured us), they met anyway. The father got wind of it, Donald was lured to a false rendezvous and thus taken. Condemned to die, he begged to be beheaded like a gentleman, rather than hanged as a felon. This request was granted, and the young man led to the block, repeating 'The Devil will take the Laird of Grant out of his shoes, and Donald Donn shall not be hanged'. He wasn't, and legend reports that as his severed head rolled from the block, it spoke, saying, 'Mary, lift ye my head'.

I shuddered, and Frank put an arm around me. 'There's a bit of one of his poems left,' he said quietly. 'Donald Donn's. It goes:

Tomorrow I shall be on a hill, without a head.
Have you no compassion for my sorrowful maiden,
My Mary, the fair and tender-eyed?'

I took his hand and squeezed it lightly.

As story after story of treachery, murder and violence was recounted, it seemed as though the loch had earned its sinister reputation.

'What about the monster?' I asked, peering over the side into the murky depths. It seemed entirely appropriate to such a setting.

Our guide shrugged and spat into the water.

'Weel, the loch's queer, and no mistake. There's stories, to be sure, of something old and evil that once lived in the depths. Sacrifices were made to it — kine, and sometimes even wee bairns, flung into the water in withy baskets.' He spat again. 'And some say the loch's bottomless — got a hole in the centre deeper than anything else in Scotland. On the other hand' — the guide's crinkled eyes crinkled a bit more — ' 'twas a family here from Lancashire a few years ago, cam' rushin' to the police station in Fort Augustus, screamin' as they'd seen the monster come out o' the water and hide in the bracken. Said 'twas a terrible creature, covered wi' red hair and fearsome horns, and chewin' something, wi' the blood all dripping from its mouth.' He held up a hand, stemming my horrified exclamation.

'The constable they sent to see cam' back and said, weel, bar the drippin' blood, 'twas a verra accurate description' — he paused for effect — 'of a nice Highland cow, chewin' her cud in the bracken!'

We sailed down half the length of the loch before disembarking for a late lunch. We met the car there and motored back through the Glen, observing nothing more sinister than a fox in the road, who looked up startled, a small animal of some sort hanging limp in its jaws, as we zoomed around a curve. It leaped for the side of the road and swarmed up the bank, swift as a shadow.

It was very late indeed when we finally staggered up the path to Mrs Baird's, but we clung together on the doorstep as Frank groped for the key, still laughing over the events of the day.

It wasn't until we were undressing for bed that I remembered to mention the miniature henge on Craigh na Dun to Frank. His fatigue vanished at once.

'Really? And you know where it is? How marvellous, Claire!' He beamed and began rattling through his suitcase.

'What are you looking for?'

'The alarm clock,' he replied, hauling it out.

'Whatever for?' I asked in astonishment.

'I want to be up in time to see them.'

'Who?'

'The witches.'

'Witches? Who told you there are witches?'

'The minister,' Frank answered, clearly enjoying the joke. 'His housekeeper's one of them.'

I thought of the dignified Mrs Graham and snorted derisively.

'Don't be ridiculous!'

'Well, not witches, actually. There have been

witches all over Scotland for hundreds of years – they burnt them till well into the eighteenth century – but this lot are really meant to be Druids, or something of the sort. I don't suppose it's actually a coven – not devil-worship, I don't mean. But the minister said there was a local group that still observes rituals on the old sun-feast days. He can't afford to take too much interest in such goings-on, you see, because of his position, but he's much too curious a man to ignore it altogether, either. He didn't know where the ceremonies took place, but if there's a stone circle nearby, that must be it.' He rubbed his hands together in anticipation. 'What luck!'

Getting up once in the dark to go adventuring is a lark. Twice in two days smacks of masochism.

No nice warm car with rugs and Thermoses this time, either. I stumbled sleepily up the hill behind Frank, tripping over roots and stubbing my toes on stones. It was cold and misty, and I dug my hands deeper into the pockets of my cardigan.

One final push up over the crest of the hill, and the henge was before us, the stones barely visible in the sombre light of pre-dawn. Frank stood stock-still, admiring them, while I subsided on to a convenient rock, panting.

'Beautiful,' he murmured. He crept silently to the outer edge of the ring, his shadowy figure disappearing among the larger shadows of the stones. Beautiful they were, and bloody eerie too. I shivered, and not entirely from the cold. If whoever had made them had meant them to impress, they'd known what they were doing.

Frank was back in a moment. 'No one here yet,' he whispered suddenly from behind me, making me jump. 'Come on, I've found a place we can watch from.'

The light was coming up from the east now, just a tinge of paler grey on the horizon, but enough to keep me from stumbling as Frank led me through a gap he had found in some alder bushes near the top of the path. There was a tiny clearing inside the clump of bushes, barely enough for the two of us to stand shoulder to shoulder. The path was clearly visible, though, and so was the interior of the stone circle, no more than twenty feet away. Not for the first time I wondered just what kind of work Frank had done during the war. He certainly seemed to know a lot about manoeuvring soundlessly in the dark.

Drowsy as I was, I wanted nothing more than to curl up under a cosy bush and go back to sleep. There wasn't room for that, though, so I continued to stand, peering down the steep path in search of oncoming Druids. I was getting a crick in my back and my feet ached, but it couldn't take long; the streak of light in the east had turned a pale pink, and I supposed it was less than half an hour till dawn.

The first one moved almost as silently as Frank. There was only the faintest of rattles as her feet dislodged a pebble near the crest of the hill, and then the neat grey head rose silently into sight. Mrs Graham. So it was true, then. The minister's housekeeper was sensibly dressed in tweed skirt and woolly coat, with a white bundle under one arm. She disappeared behind one of the standing stones, quiet as a ghost.

They came quite quickly after that, in ones and twos and threes, with subdued giggles and whispers on the path that were quickly shushed as they came into sight of the circle.

I recognized a few. Here came Mrs Buchanan, the postmistress, blonde hair freshly permed and the scent of Evening in Paris wafting strongly from its waves. I suppressed a laugh. So this was a modern-day Druid!

There were fifteen in all, and all women, ranging in age from Mrs Graham's sixty-odd years to a young woman in her early twenties, whom I had seen pushing a pram round the shops two days before. All of them were dressed for rough walking, with bundles beneath their arms. With a minimum of chat they disappeared behind stones or bushes, emerging empty-handed and bare-armed, completely clad in white. I caught the scent of laundry soap as one brushed by our clump of bushes, and recognized the garments as bedsheets, wrapped about the body and knotted at the shoulder.

They assembled outside the ring of stones, in a line from eldest to youngest, and stood in silence, waiting. The light in the east grew stronger and the line of women began to move, walking slowly between two of the stones. The leader took them directly to the centre of the circle and led them round and round, still moving slowly, stately as swans in a circular procession.

The leader suddenly stopped, raised her arms and stepped into the centre of the circle. Raising her face towards the pair of easternmost stones, she called out in a high voice. Not loud, but clear enough to be heard throughout the circle. The still mist caught the words and made them echo as though they came from all around, from the stones themselves.

Whatever the call was, it was echoed again by the dancers. For dancers they now became. Not touching, but with arms outstretched towards each other, they bobbed and weaved, still moving in a circle. Suddenly the circle split in half. Seven of the dancers moved clockwise, still in a circular motion. The others moved in the opposite direction. The two semicircles passed each other at increasing speeds, sometimes forming a complete circle, sometimes a double line. And in the centre, the leader stood stock-still, giving again and again that mournful high-pitched call, in a language long since dead.

They should have been ridiculous, and perhaps they were. A collection of women in bedsheets, many of them stout and far from agile, parading in circles on top of a hill. But the hair prickled on the back of my neck at the sound of their call.

They stopped as one and turned to face the rising sun, standing in the form of two semicircles with a path lying clear between the halves of the circle thus formed. As the sun rose above the horizon its light flooded between the eastern stones, knifed between the halves of the circle and struck the great split stone on the opposite side of the henge.

The dancers stood for a moment, frozen in the shadows to either side of the beam of light. Then Mrs Graham said something in the same strange language, but this time in a speaking voice. She pivoted and walked, back straight, iron-grey waves glinting in the sun, along the path of light. Without a word the dancers fell in step behind her. They passed one by one through the cleft in the main stone and disappeared in silence.

We crouched in the alders until the women, now laughing and chatting normally, had retrieved their clothes and set off in a group down the hill, headed for coffee at the manse.

'Goodness!' I stretched, trying to get the kinks out of my legs and back. 'That was quite a sight, wasn't it?'

'Wonderful!' enthused Frank. 'I wouldn't have missed it for the world.' He slipped out of the bush like a snake, leaving me to disentangle myself while he cast about the interior of the circle, nose to the ground like a bloodhound.

'Whatever are you looking for?' I asked. I entered the circle with some hesitation, but day was fully come and the stones, while still impressive, had lost a good deal of the brooding menace of dawn light.

'Marks,' he replied, crawling about on hands and knees, eyes intent on the short turf. 'How did they know where to start and stop?'

'Good question. I don't see anything.' Casting an eye over the ground, though, I did see an interesting plant growing near the base of one of the tall stones. Myosotis? No, probably not; this had orange centres to the deep blue flowers. Intrigued, I started towards it. Frank, with keener hearing than I, leaped to his feet and seized my arm, hurrying me out of the circle a moment before one of the morning's dancers entered from the other side.

It was Miss Grant, the tubby little woman who, suitably enough in view of her figure, ran the sweets and pastries shop in the High Street. She peered nearsightedly around, then fumbled in her pocket for her spectacles. Jamming these on her nose, she strolled about the circle, at last pouncing on the lost hair-clip for which she had returned. Having restored it to its place in her thick, glossy locks, she seemed in no hurry to return to business. Instead she seated herself on a boulder, leaned back against one of the stone giants in comradely fashion and lighted a leisurely cigarette.

Frank gave a muted sigh of exasperation beside me. 'Well,' he said, resigned, 'we'd best go. She could sit there all morning, by the looks of her. And I didn't see any obvious markings in any case.'

'Perhaps we could come back later,' I suggested, still curious about the blue-flowered plant.

'Yes, all right.' But he had plainly lost interest in the circle itself, being now absorbed in the details of the ceremony. He quizzed me relentlessly on the way down the path, urging me to remember as closely as I could the exact wording of the calls and the timing of the dance.

'Norse,' he said at last, with satisfaction. 'The root words are Ancient Norse, I'm almost sure of it. But the dance –' He shook his head, pondering. 'No, the dance is very much older. Not that there aren't Viking circle dances,' he said, raising his brows censoriously as though I had suggested there weren't. 'But that shifting pattern with the double-line business, that's . . . hmm, it's like . . . well, some of the patterns on the Beaker Folk glazeware show a pattern rather like that, but then again . . . hmm.'

He dropped into one of his scholarly trances, muttering to himself from time to time. The trance was broken only when he stumbled unexpectedly over an obstacle near the bottom of the hill. He flung his arms out with a startled cry as his feet went out from under him and he rolled untidily down the last few feet of the path, fetching up in a clump of cow parsley.

I dashed down the hill after him but found him already sitting up among the quivering stems by the time I reached the bottom.

'Are you all right?' I asked, though I could see that he was.

'I think so.' He passed a hand dazedly over his brow, smoothing back the dark hair. 'What did I trip over?'

'This.' I held up a sardine tin, discarded by some earlier visitor. 'One of the menaces of civilization.'

'Ah.' He took it from me, peered inside, then tossed it over one shoulder. 'Pity it's empty. I'm feeling rather hungry after that excursion. Shall we see what Mrs Baird can provide in the way of a late breakfast?'

'We might,' I said, smoothing the last strands of hair for him. 'And then again, we might make it an early lunch instead.' My eyes met his.

'Ah,' he said again, with a completely different tone. He ran a hand slowly up my arm and up the side of my neck, his thumb gently tickling the lobe of my ear. 'So we might.'

'If you aren't too hungry,' I said. The other hand found its way behind my back. Palm spread, it pressed me gently towards him, fingers stroking lower and lower. His mouth opened slightly and he breathed, ever so lightly, down the neck of my dress, his warm breath tickling the tops of my breasts.

He laid me carefully back in the grass, the feathery blossoms of the cow parsley seeming to float in the air around his head. He bent forward and kissed me softly, and kept on kissing me as he unbuttoned my dress, one button at a time, teasing, pausing to reach a hand inside and play with the swelling tips of my breasts. At last he had the dress laid open from neck to waist.

'Ah,' he said again, in yet another tone. 'Like white velvet.' He spoke hoarsely, and his hair had fallen forward again, but he made no attempt to brush it back.

He sprang the clasp of my brassiere with one accomplished flick of the thumb, and bent to pay a skilled homage to my breasts. Then he drew back, and cupping my breasts with both hands, drew his palms slowly down to meet between the rising mounds, and without stopping drew them softly outwards again, tracing the line of my rib cage clear to the back. Up and again, down and around, until I moaned and turned towards him. He sank his lips on to mine and pressed me towards him until our hips fitted tightly together. He bent his head to mine, nibbling softly around the rim of my ear.

The hand stroking my back slipped lower and lower, stopping suddenly in surprise. It felt again, then Frank raised his head and looked down at me, grinning.

'What's all this, then?' he asked, in imitation of a village bobby. 'Or rather, what's *not* all this?'

'Just being prepared,' I said primly. 'Nurses are taught to anticipate contingencies.'

'Really, Claire,' he murmured, sliding his hand under my skirt and up my thigh to the soft, unprotected warmth between my legs, 'you are the most terrifyingly practical person I have ever known.'

Frank came up behind me as I sat in the parlour chair that evening, a large book spread out on my lap.

'What are you doing?' he asked. His hands rested gently on my shoulders.

'Looking for that plant,' I answered, sticking a finger between the pages to mind my place. 'The one I saw in the stone circle. See . . .' I flipped the book open. 'It could be in the Gentianaceae, the Polemoniaceae, the Boraginaceae – that's most likely, I think, forget-me-nots – but it could even be a variant of this one, the Anemone patens.' I pointed out a full-colour illustration of a Pasque flower. 'I don't think it was a gentian of any kind; the petals weren't really rounded, but –'

'Well, why not go back and get it?' he suggested. 'Mr Crook would lend you his old banger, perhaps, or – no, I've a better idea. Borrow Mrs Baird's bicycle, it's safer. It's a short walk from the road to the foot of the hill.'

'And then about a thousand yards, straight up,' I said. 'Why are you so interested in that plant?' I swivelled around to look up at him. The parlour lamp outlined his head with a thin gold line, like a medieval engraving of a saint.

'It's not the plant I care about. But if you're going up there anyway, I wish you'd have a quick look around the outside of the stone circle.'

'All right,' I said obligingly. 'What for?'

'Traces of fire,' he said. 'In all the things I've been able to read about Beltane, fire is always mentioned in the rituals, yet the women we saw this morning weren't using any. I wondered if perhaps they'd set the Beltane fire the night before, then come back in the morning for the dance. Though historically it's the cowherds who were supposed to set the fire. There wasn't any trace of fire inside the circle,' he added. 'But we left before I thought of checking the outside.'

'All right,' I said again, and yawned. Two early risings in two days were taking their toll. I shut the book and stood up. 'Provided I don't have to get up before nine.'

It was in fact nearly eleven before I reached the stone circle. It was drizzling and I was soaked through, not having thought to bring a mac. I made a cursory examination of the outside of the circle, but if there had ever been a fire there, someone had taken pains to remove its traces.

The plant was easier to find. It was where I remembered it, near the foot of the tallest stone. I took several clippings of the plant and stowed them temporarily in my handkerchief, meaning to deal with them properly when I got back to Mrs Baird's bicycle, where I had left the plant press.

The tallest stone of the circle was cleft, with a vertical split dividing the two massive pieces. Oddly, the pieces had been drawn apart by some means. Though you could see that the facing surfaces matched, they were separated by a gap of two or three feet.

There was a deep humming noise coming from somewhere near at hand. I thought there might be a beehive lodged in some crevice of the rock, and placed a hand on the stone in order to lean into the cleft.

The stone screamed.

I backed away as fast as I could, moving so quickly

that I tripped on the short turf and sat down hard. I stared at the stone, sweating.

I had never heard such a sound from anything living. There is no way to describe it, except to say that it was the sort of scream you might expect from a stone. It was horrible.

The other stones began to shout. There was a noise of battle, and the cries of dying men and shattered horses.

I shook my head violently to clear it, but the noise went on. I stumbled to my feet and staggered towards the edge of the circle. The sounds were all around me, making my teeth ache and my head spin. My vision began to blur.

I do not know now whether I went deliberately towards the cleft in the main stone, or whether it was accidental, a blind drifting through the fog of noise.

Once, travelling at night, I fell asleep in the passenger seat of a moving car, lulled by the noise and motion into an illusion of serene weightlessness. The driver of the car took a bridge too fast and lost control, and I woke from my floating dream straight into the glare of headlights and the sickening sensation of falling at high speed. That abrupt transition is as close as I can come to describing the feeling I experienced, but it falls woefully short.

I could say that my field of vision contracted to a single dark spot, then disappeared altogether, leaving

not darkness but a bright void. I could say that I felt
as though I were spinning, or as though I were being
pulled inside out. All these things are true, yet none
of them conveys the sense I had of complete disrup-
tion, of being slammed very hard against something
that wasn't there.

The truth is that nothing moved, nothing changed,
nothing whatever appeared to *happen* and yet I experienced a feeling of elemental terror so great that I lost
all sense of who or what or where I was. I was in the
heart of chaos, and no power of mind or body was of
use against it.

I cannot really say I lost consciousness, but I was
certainly not aware of myself for some time. I 'woke',
if that's the word, when I stumbled on a rock near the
bottom of the hill. I half slid the remaining few feet
and fetched up on the thick tufted grass at the foot.

I felt sick and dizzy. I crawled towards a stand of
saplings and leaned against one to steady myself.
There was a confused noise of shouting nearby,
which reminded me of the sounds I had heard, and
felt, in the stone circle. The ring of inhuman violence
was lacking, though; this was the normal sound of
human conflict, and I turned towards it.

3

The Man in the Wood

The men were some distance away when I saw them. Two or three, dressed in kilts, running like the dickens across a small clearing. There was a far-off banging noise that I rather dazedly identified as gunshots. I was quite sure I was still hallucinating when the sound of shots was followed by the appearance of five or six men dressed in red coats and knee breeches, waving muskets. I blinked and stared. I moved my hand before my face and held up two fingers. I saw two fingers, all present and correct. No blurring of vision. I sniffed the air cautiously. The pungent odour of trees in spring and a faint whiff of clover from a clump near my feet. No olfactory delusions.

I felt my head. No soreness anywhere. Concussion unlikely then. Pulse a little fast, but steady.

The sound of distant yelling changed abruptly. There was a thunder of hooves, and several ponies came charging in my direction, kilted Scots atop them, yodelling in Gaelic. I dodged out of the way with an agility that seemed to prove I had not been physically damaged, whatever my mental state.

And then it came to me, as one of the redcoats, knocked flat by a fleeing Scot, rose and shook his fist theatrically after the ponies. Of course. A film! I shook my head at my own slowness. They were shooting a costume drama of some sort, that was all. One of those Bonnie-Prince-in-the-heather sorts of things, no doubt.

Well. Regardless of artistic merit, the film crew wouldn't thank me for introducing a note of historic inauthenticity into their shots. I doubled back into the wood, meaning to make a wide circle around the clearing and come out on the road where I had left the bike. The going was more difficult than I had expected, though. The wood was a young one, and dense with underbrush that snagged my clothes. I had to go carefully through the spindly saplings, disentangling my skirts from brambles as I went.

Had he been a snake I would have stepped on him. He stood so quietly among the saplings as almost to have been one of them, and I did not see him until a hand shot out and gripped me by the arm.

Its companion clapped over my mouth as I was

dragged backwards into a grove, thrashing wildly in panic. My captor, whoever he was, seemed not much taller than I, but rather noticeably strong in the forearms. I smelled a faint flowery scent, as of lavender water, and something more spicy, mingled with the sharper reek of male perspiration. As the leaves whipped back into place in the path of our passage, though, I noticed something familiar about the hand and forearm clasped about my waist.

I shook my head free of the restraint over my mouth.

'Frank!' I burst out. 'What in heaven's name are you playing at?' I was torn between relief at finding him here and irritation at the horseplay. Unsettled as I was by my experience among the stones, I was in no mood for rough games.

The hands released me, but even as I turned to him I sensed something wrong. It was not only the unfamiliar cologne but something more subtle. I stood stock-still, feeling the hair prickle on my neck.

'You aren't Frank,' I whispered.

'I am not,' he agreed, surveying me with considerable interest. 'Though I've a cousin of that name. I doubt, though, that it's he you have confused me with, madam. We do not resemble one another greatly.'

Whatever this man's cousin looked like, the man himself might have been Frank's brother. There was the same lithe, spare build and fine-drawn bones; the same chiselled lines of the face; the level brows and wide hazel eyes; and the same dark hair, curved smooth across the brow.

But this man's hair was long, tied back from his face with a leather thong. And the gypsy skin showed the deep-baked tan of months, no, years of exposure to the weather, not the light golden colour Frank's had attained during our Scottish holiday.

'Just who are you?' I demanded, feeling most uneasy. While Frank had numerous relatives and connections, I thought I knew all the British branch of the family. Certainly there was no one who looked like this man among them. And surely Frank would have mentioned any near relative living in the Highlands? Not only mentioned him but insisted upon visiting him as well, armed with the usual collection of genealogical charts and notebooks, eager for any tidbits of family history about the famous Black Jack Randall.

The stranger raised his brows at my question.

'Who am I? I might ask the same question, madam, and with considerably more justification.' His eyes raked me slowly from head to toe, travelling with a sort of insolent appreciation over the thin sprigged cotton dress I wore, and lingering with an odd look of amusement on my legs. I did not at all understand the look, but it made me extremely nervous, and I backed up a step or two until I was brought up sharp by bumping into a tree.

The man finally removed his gaze and turned aside. It was as though he had taken a constraining hand off me, and I let out my breath in relief, not realizing until then that I had been holding it.

He had turned to pick up his coat, thrown across the lowest branch of a sapling. He brushed some scattered leaves from it and began to put it on.

I must have gasped, because he looked up again. The coat was deep scarlet, long-tailed and without lapels, frogged down the front. The buff linings of the turned-back cuffs extended a good six inches up the sleeve, and a small coil of gold braid gleamed from one epaulette. It was a dragoon's coat, an officer's coat. Then it occurred to me – of course, he was an actor, from the company I had seen on the other side of the wood. Though the sword he proceeded to strap on seemed remarkably more realistic than any prop I had ever seen.

I pressed myself against the bark of the tree behind me and found it reassuringly solid. I crossed my arms protectively in front of me.

'Who the bloody hell are you?' I demanded again. The question this time came out in a croak that sounded frightened even to my ears.

As though not hearing me, he ignored the question, taking his time in the fastening of the frogs down the front of his coat. Only when he finished did he turn his attention to me once more. He bowed sardonically, hand over his heart.

'I am, madam, Jonathan Randall, Esquire, Captain of His Majesty's Eighth Dragoons. At your service, madam.'

I broke and ran. My breath rasped in my chest as I tore through the screen of alder, ignoring brambles, nettles, stones, fallen logs, everything in my path. I heard a shout behind me but was much too panicked to determine its direction.

I fled blindly, branches scratching my face and arms, ankles turning as I stepped in holes and stumbled on rocks. I had no room in my mind for any form of rational thought; I wanted only to get away from him.

A heavy weight struck me hard in the lower back and I pitched forward at full length, landing with a thud that knocked the wind out of me. Rough hands flipped me on to my back, and Captain Jonathan Randall rose to his knees above me. He was breathing heavily and had lost his sword in the chase. He looked dishevelled, dirty and thoroughly annoyed.

'What the devil do you mean by running away like that?' he demanded. A thick lock of dark brown hair had come loose and curved across his brow, making him look even more disconcertingly like Frank.

He leaned down and grasped me by the arms. Still

gasping for breath, I struggled to get free but succeeded only in dragging him down on top of me.

He lost his balance and collapsed at full length on me, flattening me once more. Surprisingly enough, this seemed to make his annoyance vanish.

'Oh, like that, is it?' he said, with a chuckle. 'Well, I'd be most willing to oblige you, Chuckie, but it happens you've chosen a rather inopportune moment.' His weight pressed my hips to the ground and a small rock was digging painfully into the small of my back. I squirmed to dislodge it. He ground his hips hard against mine and his hands pinned my shoulders to the earth. My mouth fell open in outrage.

'What do you . . .' I began, but he ducked his head and kissed me, cutting short my expostulations. His tongue thrust into my mouth and explored me with a bold familiarity, roving and plunging, retreating and lunging again. Then, just as suddenly as he had begun, he pulled back.

He patted my cheek. 'Quite nice, Chuckie. Perhaps later, when I've the leisure to attend to you properly.'

I had by this time recovered my breath, and I used it. I screamed directly into his earhole, and he jerked as though I had run a hot wire into it. I took advantage of the movement to get my knee up, and jabbed it into his exposed side, sending him sprawling into the leaf mould.

I scrambled awkwardly to my feet. He rolled expertly and came up alongside me. I glanced wildly around, looking for a way out, but we were flush up against the foot of one of those towering cliffs that jut so abruptly from the soil of the Scottish Highlands. He had caught me at a point where the rock face broke inwards, forming a shallow stony box. He blocked the entrance to the declivity, arms spread and braced between the rock walls, an expression of mingled anger and curiosity on his handsome dark face.

'Who were you with?' he demanded. 'Frank, whoever he is? I've no man by that name among my company. Or is it some man who lives nearby?' He smiled derisively. 'You haven't the smell of dung on your skin, so you haven't been with a cottar. For that matter, you look a bit more expensive than the local farmers could afford.'

I clenched my fists and set my chin. Whatever this joker had in mind, I was having none of it.

'I haven't the faintest idea what you are talking about, and I'll thank you to let me pass at once!' I said, adopting my very best ward-sister's tone. This generally had a good effect on recalcitrant orderlies and junior doctors, but appeared merely to amuse Captain Randall. I was resolutely repressing the feelings of fear and disorientation that were flapping under my ribs like a panicked flock of hens.

He shook his head slowly, examining me once more in detail.

'Not just at present, Chuckie. I'm asking myself,' he said conversationally, 'just why a whore abroad in her shift would be wearing her shoes? And quite fine ones, at that,' he added, glancing at my plain brown flatties.

'A what!' I exclaimed.

He ignored me completely. His gaze had returned to my face, and he suddenly stepped forward and gripped my chin in his hand. I grabbed his wrist and yanked.

'Let go of me!' He had fingers like steel. Disregarding my efforts to free myself, he turned my face from one side to the other, so the fading afternoon light shone on it.

'The skin of a lady, I'll swear,' he murmured to himself. He leaned forward and sniffed. 'And a French scent in your hair.' He let go then, and I rubbed my jaw indignantly, as though to erase the touch I still felt on my skin.

'The rest might be managed with money from your patron,' he mused, 'but you've the speech of a lady too.'

'Thanks so much!' I snapped. 'Get out of my way. My husband is expecting me; if I'm not back in ten minutes, he'll come looking for me.'

'Oh, your husband?' The derisively admiring expression retreated somewhat, but did not disappear completely. 'And what is your husband's name, pray? Where is he? And why does he allow his wife to wander alone through deserted woods in a state of undress?'

I had been throttling that part of my brain that was beating itself to pieces trying to make sense of the whole afternoon. It now managed to break through long enough to tell me that however absurd I thought its conjectures, giving this man Frank's name, the same as his own, was only likely to lead to further trouble. Disdaining therefore to answer him, I made to push past him. He blocked my passage with a muscular arm and reached for me with his other hand.

There was a sudden whoosh from above, followed immediately by a blur before my eyes and a dull thud. Captain Randall was on the ground at my feet, under a heaving mass that looked like a bundle of old tartan rags. A brown rocklike fist rose out of the mass and descended with considerable force, meeting decisively with some bony protuberance, by the sound of the resultant crack. The Captain's struggling legs, shiny in tall brown boots, relaxed quite suddenly.

I found myself staring into a pair of sharp black eyes. The sinewy hand that had temporarily distracted the Captain's unwelcome attentions was attached like a limpet to my forearm.

'And who the hell are you?' I said in astonishment. My rescuer, if I cared to call him that, was some inches shorter than I and sparely built, but the bare arms protruding from the ragged shirt were knotted with muscle and his whole frame gave the impression of being made of some resilient material such as bed-springs. No beauty, either, with a pockmarked skin, low brow and narrow jaw.

'This way.' He jerked on my arm, and I, stupefied by the rush of recent events, obediently followed.

My new companion pushed his way rapidly through a scrim of alder, made an abrupt turn around a large rock, and suddenly we were on a path. Over-grown with gorse and heather, and zigzagging so that it was never visible for more than six feet ahead, it was still unmistakably a path, leading steeply up towards the crest of a hill.

Not until we were picking our way cautiously down the far side of the hill did I gather breath and wit enough to ask where we were going. Receiving no answer from my companion, I repeated, 'Where on earth are we going?' in a louder tone.

To my considerable surprise he rounded on me, face contorted, and pushed me off the path. As I opened my mouth to protest he clapped a hand over it and dragged me to the ground, rolling on top of me.

Not again! I thought, and was heaving desperately

to and fro to free myself when I heard what he had heard, and suddenly lay still. Voices called back and forth, accompanied by trampling and splashing sounds. They were unmistakably English voices. I struggled violently to get my mouth free. I sank my teeth into his hand, and had time only to register the fact that he had been eating pickled herring with his fingers, before something crashed against the back of my skull, and everything went dark.

The stone cottage loomed up suddenly through a haze of night mist. The shutters were bolted tight, showing no more than a thread of light. Having no idea how long I had been travelling, I couldn't tell how far this place was from the hill of Craigh na Dun or the town of Inverness. We were on horse-back, myself mounted before my captor with hands tied to the pommel, but there was no road, so progress was still rather slow.

I thought I had not been out for long; I showed no symptoms of concussion or other ill effects from the blow, save a sore patch on the base of my skull. My captor, a man of few words, had responded to my questions, demands and acerbic remarks alike with the all-purpose Scottish noise which can best be rendered phonetically as 'Mmmphm'. Had I been in any doubt as to his nationality, that sound alone would have been sufficient to remove it.

My eyes had gradually adapted to the dwindling light as the pony stumbled through the stones and gorse, so it was a shock to step from near-dark into what seemed a blaze of light inside. As the dazzle receded I could see that in fact the single room was lit only by a fire, several candlesticks and a dangerously old-fashioned-looking oil lamp.

'What is it ye have there, Murtagh?'

The weasel-faced man grabbed me by the arm and urged me blinking into the firelight.

'A Sassenach wench, by her speech.' There were several men in the room, all apparently staring at me, some in curiosity, some with unmistakable leers. My dress had been torn in various spots during the afternoon's activities, and I hastily took stock of the damage. Looking down, I could see the curve of one breast clearly through a rip, and I was sure the assembled men could too. I decided that making an attempt to pull the torn edges together would only draw further attention to the prospect; instead I chose a face at random and stared boldly at him, in hopes of distracting either the man or myself.

'Eh, a bonny one, Sassenach or no,' said the man, a fat, greasy sort with a black beard, seated by the fire. He was holding a chunk of bread and didn't bother to set it down as he rose and came over to me. He pushed my chin up with the back of his hand, shoving the hair out of my face. A few breadcrumbs fell down the neck of my dress. The other men clustered close around, a mass of tartan and whiskers, smelling strongly of sweat and alcohol. It was only then that I saw they were all kilted – odd, even for this part of the Highlands. Had I stumbled into the meeting of a clan society, or perhaps a regimental reunion?

'C'mere, lass.' A large, dark-bearded man remained seated at the table by the window as he beckoned me. By his air of command, he seemed to be the leader of this pack. The men parted reluctantly as Murtagh pulled me forward, apparently respecting his rights as captor.

The dark man looked me over carefully, no expression on his face. He was good-looking, I thought, and not unfriendly. There were lines of strain between his brows, though, and it wasn't a face one would willingly cross.

'What's your name, lass?' His voice was light for a man of his size, not the deep bass I would have expected from the barrel chest.

'Claire . . . Claire Beauchamp,' I said, deciding on the spur of the moment to use my maiden name. If it were ransom they had in mind, I didn't want to help them by giving a name that could lead to Frank. And I wasn't sure I wanted these rough-looking men to know who I was, before I found out who they were.

'And just what do you think you're —' The dark man ignored me, establishing a pattern that I was to grow tired of very quickly.

'Beauchamp?' The heavy brows lifted and the general company stirred in surprise. 'A French name, it is, surely?' He had in fact pronounced the name in correct French, though I had given it the common English pronunciation of 'Beecham'.

'Yes, that's right,' I answered in some surprise.

'Where did ye find this lass?' he demanded, swinging round on Murtagh, who was refreshing himself from a leather flask.

The swarthy little man shrugged. 'At the foot o' Craigh na Dun, Dougal. She was havin' words with a certain captain of dragoons wi' whom I chanced to be acquent',' he added, with a significant lift of his eyebrows. 'There seemed to be some question as to whether the lady was or was not a whore.'

Dougal looked me over carefully once more, taking in every detail of cotton print dress and walking shoes.

'I see. And what was the lady's position in this discussion?' he inquired, with a sarcastic emphasis on the 'lady' that I didn't particularly care for. I noticed that while his Scots was less pronounced than that of the man called Murtagh, his accent was still broad enough that the word was almost, though not quite, 'leddy'.

Murtagh seemed grimly amused; at least one corner of the thin mouth turned up. 'She said she wasna.
The Captain himself appeared to be of two minds
on the matter, but inclined to put the question to
the test.'

'We could do the same, come to that.' The fat,
black-bearded man stepped towards me grinning,
hands tugging at his belt. I backed up hastily as far
as I could, which was not nearly far enough, given the
dimensions of the cottage.

'That will do, Rupert.' Dougal was still scowling
at me, but his voice held the ring of authority, and
Rupert stopped his advances, making a comical face
of disappointment.

'I don't hold wi' rape, and we've not the time for it,
anyway.' I was pleased to hear this statement of policy, dubious as its moral underpinning might be, but
remained a bit nervous in the face of the openly
lascivious looks on some of the other faces. I felt
absurdly as though I had appeared in public in my
undergarments. And while I had no idea who or what
these Highland bandits were up to, they seemed
bloody dangerous. I bit my tongue, repressing a number of more or less injudicious remarks that were
bubbling towards the surface.

'What d'ye say, Murtagh?' Dougal demanded of
my captor. 'She doesna appear to care for Rupert, at
least.'

'That's no proof,' objected a short, squint-eyed man. 'He didna offer her any siller. Ye canna expect any woman to take on something like Rupert without substantial payment – in advance,' he added, to the considerable hilarity of his companions. Dougal stilled the racket with an abrupt gesture, though, and jerked his head towards the door. Squint-eye, still grinning, obediently slid out into the darkness.

Murtagh, who had not joined in the laughter, was frowning as he looked me over. He shook his head, making the lank fringe across his forehead sway.

'Nay,' he said definitely. 'I've no idea what she might be – or who – but I'll stake my best shirt she's no whore.' I hoped in that case that his best was not the one he was wearing, which scarcely looked worth the wagering.

'Weel, ye'd know, Murtagh, ye've seen enough o' them,' gibed Rupert, but was gruffly hushed by Dougal.

'We'll puzzle it out later,' said Dougal brusquely. 'We've a good distance to go tonight, and we mun' do something for Jamie first; he canna ride like that.'

I shrank back into the shadows near the fireplace, hoping to avoid notice. The man called Murtagh had untied my hands before leading me in here. Perhaps I could slip away while they were busy elsewhere. The men's attention had shifted to a young man crouched on a stool in the corner. He had barely looked up through my appearance and interrogation but kept his head bent, hand clutching the opposite shoulder, rocking slightly back and forth in pain.

Dougal gently pushed the clutching hand away. One of the men pulled back the young man's plaid, revealing a dirt-smeared linen shirt blotched with blood. A small man with a balding head came up behind the lad with a single-bladed knife, and holding the shirt at the collar, slit it across the breast and down the sleeve, so that it fell away from the shoulder.

I gasped, as did several of the men. The shoulder had been wounded; there was a deep ragged furrow across the top, and blood was running freely down the young man's breast. But more shocking was the shoulder joint itself. A dreadful hump rose on that side, and the arm hung at an impossible angle.

Dougal grunted. 'Mmph. Out o' joint, poor bugger.' The young man looked up for the first time. Though drawn with pain and stubbled with red beard, it was a strong, good-humoured face.

'Fell wi' my hand out, when the musket ball knocked me off my saddle. I landed with all my weight on the hand, and *crunch!* there it went.'

'Crunch is right.' The bald man – a Scot, and educated, to judge by his accent – was probing the shoulder, making the lad grimace in pain. 'The wound's no trouble. The ball went right through, and it's clean — the blood's runnin' free enough.' The man picked up a wad of grimy cloth from the table and used it to blot the blood. 'I don't know quite what to do about the disjointure, though. We'd need a chirurgeon to put it back in place properly. You canna ride with it that way, can you, Jamie lad?'

Musket ball? I thought blankly. *Chirurgeon?*

The young man shook his head, white-faced. 'Hurts bad enough sitting still. I couldna manage a pony.' He squeezed his eyes shut and set his teeth in his lower lip.

Murtagh spoke impatiently. 'Well, we canna leave him behind noo, can we? The lobsterbacks are no great shakes trackin' in the dark, but they'll find this place sooner or later, shutters or no. And Jamie can hardly pass for an innocent cottar, wi' yon great hole in 'im.'

'Dinna worry yourself,' Dougal said shortly. 'I don't mean to be leaving him behind.'

The bald man sighed. 'No help for it, then. We'll have to try and force the joint back. Murtagh, you and Rupert hold him; I'll give it a try.'

I watched in sympathy as he picked up the young man's arm by wrist and elbow and began forcing it upwards. The angle was quite wrong; it must be causing agonizing pain. Sweat poured down the young man's face but he made no sound beyond a soft groan. Suddenly he slumped forward, kept from

falling on the floor only by the grip of the men holding him.

One unstoppered a leather flask and pressed it to
his lips. The reek of the raw spirit reached me where
I stood. The young man coughed and gagged but
swallowed nonetheless, dribbling the amber liquid
on to the remains of his shirt.

'All right for another go, lad?' the bald man asked.
'Or maybe Rupert should have a try,' he suggested,
turning to the squat, black-bearded ruffian.

Rupert, so invited, flexed his shoulders as though
to toss a caber, and picked up the young man's wrist,
plainly intending to put the joint back by main force;
an operation, it was clear, which was likely to snap
the arm like a broomstick.

'Don't you dare to do that!' All thought of escape
submerged in professional outrage, I started forward,
oblivious to the startled looks of the men around me.

'What do you mean?' snapped the bald man,
clearly irritated by my intrusion.

'I mean that you'll break his arm if you do it like
that,' I snapped back. 'Stand out of the way, please.' I
elbowed Rupert back and took hold of the patient's
wrist myself. The patient looked as surprised as the
rest, but didn't resist. His skin was very warm, but
not feverish, I judged.

'You have to get the bone of the upper arm at the
proper angle before it will slip back into its joint,'

I said, grunting as I pulled the wrist up and the elbow in. The young man was sizable; his arm was heavy as lead.

'This is the worst part,' I warned the patient. I cupped the elbow, ready to whip it upwards and in.

His mouth twitched, not quite a smile. 'It canna hurt much worse than it does. Get on wi' it.' Sweat was popping out on my own face by now. Resetting a shoulder joint is hard work at the best of times. Done on a large man who had gone hours since the dislocation, his muscles now swollen and pulling on the joint, the job was taking all the strength I had. The fire was dangerously close; I hoped we wouldn't both topple in, if the joint went back with a jerk.

Suddenly the shoulder gave a soft crunching *pop!* and the joint was back in place. The patient looked amazed. He put an unbelieving hand up to explore.

'It doesna hurt any more!' A broad grin of delighted relief spread across his face, and the men broke out in exclamations and applause.

'It will.' I was sweating from the exertion, but smugly pleased with the results. 'It will be tender for several days. You mustn't extend the joint at all for two or three days; when you do use it again, go very slowly at first. Stop at once if it begins to hurt, and use warm compresses on it daily.'

I became aware, in the midst of this advice, that while the patient was listening respectfully the other men were eyeing me with looks ranging from wonder to outright suspicion.

'I'm a nurse, you see,' I explained, feeling somehow defensive.

Dougal's eyes, and Rupert's as well, dropped to my bosom and fastened there with a sort of horrified fascination. They exchanged glances, then Dougal looked back at my face.

'Be that as it may,' he said, raising his brows at me. 'For a wetnurse, you'd seem to have some skill at healing. Can ye stanch the lad's wound, well enough for him to sit a horse?'

'I can dress the wound, yes,' I said with considerable asperity. 'Provided you've anything to dress it with. But just what do you mean by "wetnurse"? And why do you suppose I'd want to help you, anyway?'

I was ignored as Dougal turned and spoke in a tongue I dimly recognized as Gaelic to a woman who cowered in the corner. Surrounded by the mass of men, I had not noticed her before. She was dressed oddly, I thought, in a long, ragged skirt and a long-sleeved blouse half covered by a sort of bodice or jerkin. Everything was rather on the grubby side, including her face. Glancing around, though, I could see that the cottage lacked not only electricity but also indoor plumbing; perhaps there was some excuse for the dirt.

The woman bobbed a quick curtsy, and scuttling

past Rupert and Murtagh, she began digging in a painted wooden chest by the hearth, emerging finally with a pile of ratty cloths.

'No, that won't do,' I said, fingering them gingerly. 'The wound needs to be disinfected first, then bandaged with a clean cloth, if there are no sterile bandages.'

Eyebrows rose all round. 'Disinfected?' said the small man carefully.

'Yes, indeed,' I said firmly, thinking him a bit simpleminded, in spite of his educated accent. 'All dirt must be removed from the wound and it must be treated with a compound to discourage germs and promote healing.'

'Such as?'

'Such as iodine,' I said. Seeing no comprehension on the faces before me, I tried again. 'Dilute carbolic? Or perhaps even just alcohol?' Looks of relief. At last I had found a word they appeared to recognize. Murtagh thrust the leather flask into my hands. I sighed with impatience. I knew the Highlands were primitive, but this was nearly unbelievable.

'Look,' I said, as patiently as I could. 'Why don't you just take him down into the town? It can't be far, and I'm sure there's a doctor there who could see to him.'

The woman gawped at me. 'What town?'

The big man called Dougal was ignoring this

discussion, peering cautiously into the darkness through the shutter's crack. He stepped quietly to the door, and the men fell quiet as he vanished into the night.

In a moment he was back, bringing the squint-eyed man and the cold sharp scent of dark pines with him. He shook his head in answer to the men's questioning looks.

'Nay, nothing close. We'll go at once, while it's safe.'

Catching sight of me, he stopped for a moment, thinking. Suddenly he nodded at me, decision made.

'She'll come with us,' he said. He rummaged in the pile of cloths on the table and came up with a tattered rag; it looked like a neckcloth that had seen better days.

The bald man seemed disinclined to have me along, wherever they were going.

'Why do ye no just leave her here?'

Dougal cast him an impatient glance, but left it to Murtagh to explain. 'Wherever the redcoats are now, they'll be here by dawn, which is no so far off, considering. If this woman's an English spy, we canna risk leaving her here to tell them which way we've gone. And if she should not be on good terms wi' them' – he looked dubiously at me – 'we certainly canna leave a lone woman here in her shift.' He brightened a bit, fingering the fabric of my skirt. 'She might be worth a bit in the way of ransom, at that; little as she has on, it's fine stuff.'

'Besides,' Dougal added, interrupting, 'she may be useful on the way; she seems to know a bit about doctoring. But we've no time for that now. I'm afraid ye'll have to go without bein' "disinfected", Jamie,' he said, clapping the younger man on the back. 'Can ye ride one-handed?'

'Aye.'

'Good lad. Here,' he said, tossing the greasy rag at me. 'Bind up his wound, quickly. We'll be leaving directly. Do you two get the ponies,' he said, turning to weasel-face and the fat one called Rupert.

I turned the rag round distastefully.

'I can't use this,' I complained. 'It's filthy.'

Without seeing him move, I found the big man gripping my shoulder, his hazel eyes an inch from mine. 'Do it,' he said.

Freeing me with a push, he strode to the door and disappeared after his two henchmen. Feeling more than a little shaken, I turned to the task of bandaging the musket wound as best I could. The thought of using the grimy neckrag was something my medical training wouldn't let me contemplate. I tried to bury my confusion and terror in the task of trying to find something more suitable, and, after a quick and futile search through the pile of rags, finally settled on strips of rayon torn from the hem of my slip.

While hardly sterile, it was by far the cleanest material at hand.

The linen of my patient's shirt was old and worn, but still surprisingly tough. With a bit of a struggle I ripped the rest of the sleeve open and used it to improvise a sling. I stepped back to survey the results of my impromptu field dressing, and backed straight into the big man, who had come in quietly to watch.

He looked approvingly at my handiwork. 'Good job, lass. Come on, we're ready.'

Dougal handed a coin to the woman and hustled me out of the cottage, followed more slowly by Jamie, still a bit white-faced. Unfolded from the low stool, my patient proved to be quite tall; he stood several inches over Dougal, himself a tall man.

The black-bearded Rupert and Murtagh were holding six ponies outside, muttering soft Gaelic endearments to them in the dark. It was a moonless night, but the starlight caught the metal bits of the harness in flashes of quicksilver. I looked up and almost gasped in wonder; the night sky was thick with a glory of stars such as I had never seen. Glancing round at the surrounding forest, I understood. With no nearby city to veil the sky with light, the stars here held undisputed dominion over the night.

And then I stopped dead, feeling much colder than the night chill justified. No city lights. 'What town?' the woman inside had asked. Accustomed as I was to blackouts and air raids from the war years, the lack of light had not at first disturbed me. But this was peacetime, and the lights of Inverness should have been visible for miles.

The men were shapeless masses in the dark. I thought of trying to slip away into the trees, but Dougal, apparently divining my thought, grabbed my elbow and pulled me towards the ponies.

'Jamie, get yourself up,' he called. 'The lass will ride wi' you.' He squeezed my elbow. 'You can hold the reins, if Jamie canna manage one-handed, but do ye take care to keep close wi' the rest of us. Should ye try anythin' else, I shall cut your throat. D'ye understand me?'

I nodded, throat too dry to answer. His voice was not particularly threatening, but I believed every word. I was the less tempted to 'try anythin' ', in that I had no idea what to try. I didn't know where I was, who my companions were, why we were leaving with such urgency or where we were going, but I lacked any reasonable alternatives to going with them. I was worried about Frank, who must long since have started looking for me, but this didn't seem the time to mention him.

Dougal must have sensed my nod, for he let go of my arm and stooped suddenly beside me. I stood stupidly staring down at him until he hissed, 'Your foot, lass! Give me your foot! Your *left* foot,' he added disgustedly. I hastily took my misplaced right foot out of his hand and stepped up with my left. With a slight grunt, he boosted me into the saddle in front of Jamie, who gathered me in closely with his good arm.

In spite of the general awkwardness of my situation I was grateful for the young Scot's warmth. He smelt strongly of woodsmoke, blood and unwashed male, but the night chill bit through my thin dress and I was happy enough to lean back against him.

With no more than a faint chinking of bridles we moved off into the starlit night. There was no conversation among the men, only a general wary watchfulness. The ponies broke into a trot as soon as we reached the track, and I was jostled too uncomfortably to want to talk myself, even assuming that anyone was willing to listen.

My companion seemed to be having little trouble, in spite of being unable to use his right hand. I could feel his thighs behind mine, shifting and pressing occasionally to guide the pony. I clutched the edge of the short saddle in order to stay seated; I had been on horses before, but was by no means the horseman this Jamie was.

After a time we reached a cross track, where we stopped a moment while the bald man and the leader conferred in low tones. Jamie dropped the reins over the pony's neck and let it wander to the verge to crop grass, while he began twisting and turning behind me.

'Careful!' I said. 'Don't twist like that or your dressing will come off! What are you trying to do?'

'Get my plaid loose to cover you,' he replied. 'You're shivering. But I canna do it one-handed. Can ye reach the clasp of my brooch for me?'

With a good deal of tugging and awkward shifting we got the plaid loosened. With a surprisingly dexterous swirl he twirled the cloth out and let it settle, shawl-like, around his shoulders. He then put the ends over my shoulders and tucked them neatly under the saddle edge, so that we were both warmly wrapped.

'There!' he said. 'We dinna want ye to freeze before we get there.'

'Thank you,' I said, grateful for the shelter. 'But where are we going?'

I couldn't see his face, behind and above me, but he paused a moment before answering.

At last he laughed shortly. 'Tell ye the truth, lassie, I don't know. Daresay we'll both find out when we get there, eh?'

Something seemed faintly familiar about the section of countryside through which we were passing. Surely

I knew that large rock formation ahead, the one shaped like a rooster's tail?

'Cocknammon Rock!' I exclaimed.

'Aye, reckon,' said my escort, unexcited by this revelation.

'Didn't the English use it for ambushes?' I asked, trying to remember the dreary details of local history Frank had spent hours regaling me with over the last week. 'If there is an English patrol in the neighbourhood . . .' I hesitated. If there was an English patrol in the neighbourhood, perhaps I was wrong to draw attention to it. And yet, in case of an ambush, I would be quite indistinguishable from my companion, shrouded as we were in one plaid. And I thought again of Captain Jonathan Randall, and shuddered involuntarily. Everything I had seen since I had stepped through the cleft stone pointed towards the completely irrational conclusion that the man I had met in the wood was in fact Frank's six-times-great-grandfather. I fought stubbornly against this conclusion, but was unable to formulate another that met the facts.

I had at first imagined that I was merely dreaming more vividly than usual, but Randall's kiss, rudely familiar and immediately physical, had dispelled that impression. Neither did I imagine that I had dreamed being knocked on the head by Murtagh; the soreness on my scalp was being matched by a chafing of my inner thighs against the saddle, which seemed most undreamlike. And the blood; yes, I was familiar enough with blood to have dreamed of it before. But never had I dreamed the scent of blood; that warm, coppery tang that I could still smell on the man behind me.

'*Tck.*' He clucked to our mount and urged it up alongside the leader's, engaging the burly shadow in quiet Gaelic conversation. The ponies slowed to a walk.

At a signal from the leader, Jamie, Murtagh and the small bald man dropped back, while the others spurred up and galloped towards the rock, a quarter mile ahead to the right. A half moon had come up, and the light was bright enough to pick out the leaves of the bluebells growing on the trackside, but the shadows in the clefts of the rock could hide anything.

Just as the galloping shapes passed the rock, a flash of musket fire sparked from a hollow. There was a bloodcurdling shriek from directly behind me, and the pony leaped forward as though jabbed with a sharp stick. We were suddenly racing towards the rock across the heather, Murtagh and the other man alongside, hair-raising screams and bellows splitting the night air.

I hung on to the pommel for dear life. Suddenly reining up next to a large gorse bush, Jamie grabbed me round the waist and unceremoniously dumped me into it. The pony whirled sharply and sprinted off again, circling the rock to come along the south side. I could see the rider crouching low in the saddle as the pony vanished into the rock's shadow. When it emerged, still galloping, the saddle was empty.

The rock surfaces were cratered with shadow; I could hear shouts and occasional musket shots, but couldn't tell if the movements I saw were those of men, or only the shades of the stunted trees that sprouted from cracks in the rock.

I extricated myself from the bush with some difficulty, picking bits of prickly gorse from my skirt and hair. I licked a scratch on my hand, wondering what on earth I was to do now. I could wait for the battle at the rock to be decided. If the Scots won, or at least survived, I supposed they would come back looking for me. If they did not, I could approach the English, who might well assume that if I were travelling with the Scots I was in league with them. In league to do what, I had no idea, but it was quite plain from the men's behaviour at the cottage that they were up to something which they expected the English strongly to disapprove of.

Perhaps it would be better to avoid both sides in this conflict. After all, now that I knew where I was, I stood some chance of getting back to a town or village that I knew, even if I had to walk all the way.

I set off with decision towards the track, tripping over innumerable lumps of stone, the bastard offspring of Cocknammon Rock.

The moonlight made walking deceptive; though I could see every detail of the ground, I had no depth perception; flat plants and jagged stones looked the same height, causing me to lift my feet absurdly high over nonexistent obstacles and stub my toes on protruding rocks. I walked as fast as I could, listening for sounds of pursuit behind me.

The noises of battle had faded by the time I reached the track. I realized that I was too visible on the path itself, but I needed to follow it, if I were to find my way to a town. I had no sense of direction in the dark, and had never learned from Frank his trick of navigation by the stars. Thinking of Frank made me want to cry, so I tried to distract myself by trying to make sense of the day's events.

It seemed inconceivable, but all appearances pointed to my being in some place where the customs and politics of the mid-eighteenth century still held sway. I would have thought the whole thing a fancy-dress show of some type, had it not been for the injuries of the young man they called Jamie. That wound had indeed been made by something very like a musket ball, judging from the evidence it left behind. The behaviour of the men in the cottage was not consistent with any sort of play-acting, either.

They were serious men, and the dirks and swords were real.

Could it be some secluded enclave, perhaps, where the villagers re-enacted part of their history periodically? I had heard of such things in Germany, though never in Scotland. *You've never heard of the actors shooting each other with muskets, either, have you?* jeered the uncomfortably rational part of my mind.

I looked back at the rock to check my position, then ahead to the skyline, and my blood ran cold. There was nothing there but the feathered needles of pine trees, impenetrably black against the spread of stars. Where were the lights of Inverness? If that was Cocknammon Rock behind me, as I knew it was, then Inverness must be less than three miles to the southwest. At this distance I should be able to see the glow of the town against the sky. If it were there.

I shook myself irritably, hugging my elbows against the chill. Even admitting for a moment the completely implausible idea that I was in another time than my own, Inverness had stood in its present location for some six hundred years. It was there. But, apparently, it had no lights. Under the circumstances this strongly suggested that there were no electric lights to be had. Yet another piece of evidence, if I needed it. But evidence of what, exactly?

A shape stepped out of the dark so close in front of me that I nearly bumped into it. Stifling a scream

I turned to run, but a large hand gripped my arm, preventing escape.

'Dinna worry, lass. 'Tis me.'

'That's what I was afraid of,' I said crossly, though in fact I was relieved that it was Jamie. I was not so afraid of him as of the other men, though he looked just as dangerous. Still, he was young, even younger than me, I judged. And it was difficult for me to be afraid of someone I had so recently treated as a patient.

'I hope you haven't been misusing that shoulder,' I said in the rebuking voice of a hospital matron. If I could establish a sufficient tone of authority, perhaps I could persuade him into letting me go.

'Yon wee stramash didna do it any good,' he admitted, massaging the shoulder with his free hand.

Just then he moved into a patch of moonlight and I saw the huge spread of blood on his shirt front. Arterial bleeding, I thought at once; but then, why is he still standing?

'You're hurt!' I exclaimed. 'Have you broken open your shoulder wound, or is it fresh? Sit down and let me see!' I pushed him towards a pile of boulders, rapidly reviewing procedures for emergency field treatment. No supplies to hand, save what I was wearing. I was reaching for the remains of my slip, intending to use it to stanch the flow, when he laughed.

'Nay, pay it no mind, lass. This lot isna *my* blood. Not much of it, anyway,' he added, plucking the soaked fabric gingerly away from his body.

I swallowed, feeling a bit queasy. 'Oh,' I said weakly.

'Dougal and the others will be waiting by the track. Let's go.' He took me by the arm, less as a gallant gesture than a means of forcing me to accompany him. I decided to take a chance and dug in my heels.

'No! I'm not going with you!'

He stopped, surprised at my resistance. 'Yes, you are.' He didn't seem upset by my refusal; in fact, he seemed slightly amused that I had any objection to being kidnapped again.

'And what if I won't? Are you going to cut my throat?' I demanded, forcing the issue. He considered the alternatives and answered calmly.

'Why, no. You don't look heavy. If ye won't walk, I shall pick you up and sling ye over my shoulder. Do ye want me to do that?' He took a step towards me, and I hastily retreated. I hadn't the slightest doubt he would do it, injury or no.

'No! You can't do that; you'll damage your shoulder again.'

His features were indistinct but the moonlight caught the gleam of teeth as he grinned.

'Well then, since ye don't want me to hurt myself, I suppose that means as you're comin' with me?'

I struggled for an answer, but failed to find one in time. He took my arm again, firmly, and we set off towards the track.

Jamie kept a tight hold on my arm, hauling me upright when I stumbled over rocks and plants. He himself walked as though the stubbled heath were a paved road in broad daylight. He has cat blood, I reflected sourly; no doubt that was how he managed to sneak up on me in the darkness.

The other men were, as advertised, waiting with the ponies at no great distance; apparently there had been no losses or injuries, for they were all present. Scrambling up in an undignified scuffle, I plopped down in the saddle again. My head gave Jamie's bad shoulder an unintentional thump, and he drew in his breath with a hiss.

I tried to cover my resentment at being recaptured and my remorse at having hurt him with an air of bullying officiousness.

'Serves you right, brawling round the countryside and chasing through bushes and rocks. I told you not to move that joint; now you've probably got torn muscles as well as bruises.'

He seemed amused by my scolding. 'Well, it wasna much of a choice. If I'd not moved my shoulder, I wouldna have ever moved anything else again. I can handle a single redcoat wi' one hand — maybe even two of them,' he said, a bit boastfully, 'but not three.

'Besides,' he said, drawing me against his blood-encrusted shirt, 'ye can fix it for me again when we get where we're going.'

'That's what you think,' I said coldly, squirming away from the sticky fabric. He clucked to the pony and we set off again. The men were in ferocious good spirits after the fight, and there was a good deal of laughter and joking. My minor part in thwarting the ambush was much praised, and toasts were drunk in my honour from the flasks that several of the men carried.

I was offered some of the contents but declined at first on the grounds that I found it hard enough to stay in the saddle sober. From the men's discussion I gathered it had been a small patrol of some ten English soldiers, armed with muskets and sabres, the same patrol they had tangled with earlier.

Someone passed a flask to Jamie and I could smell the hot, burnt-smelling spirit as he drank. I wasn't at all thirsty, but the faint scent of honey reminded me that I was starving, and had been for some time. My stomach gave an embarrassingly loud growl, protesting my neglect.

'Hey, then, Jamie-lad! Hungry, are ye? Or have ye a set of bagpipes with ye?' shouted Rupert, mistaking the source of the noise.

'Hungry enough to eat a set of pipes, I reckon,' called Jamie, gallantly assuming the blame. A moment later, a hand with a flask came round in front of me again.

'Better have a wee nip,' he whispered to me. 'It willna fill your belly, but it will make ye forget you're hungry.'

And a number of other things as well, I hoped. I tilted the flask and swallowed.

My escort had been correct; the whisky built a small warm fire that burned comfortably in my stomach, obscuring the hunger pangs. We managed without incident for several miles, taking turns with both reins and whisky flask. Near a ruined cottage, though, the breathing of my escort gradually changed to a ragged gasping. Our precarious balance, heretofore contained in a staid wobble, suddenly became much more erratic. I was confused; if *I* wasn't drunk, it seemed rather unlikely that *he* was.

'Stop! Help!' I yelled. 'He's going over!' I remembered my last unrehearsed descent and had no inclination to repeat it.

Dark shapes swirled and crowded around us, with a confused muttering of voices. Jamie slid off headfirst like a sack of stones, luckily landing in someone's arms. The rest of the men were off their ponies and had him laid in a field by the time I had scrambled down.

'He's breathin'; said one.

'Well, how very helpful,' I snapped, groping frantically for a pulse in the blackness. I found one at last, rapid but fairly strong. Putting a hand on his chest and an ear to his mouth, I could feel a regular rise and fall, with less of that gasping note. I straightened up.

'I think he's just fainted,' I said. 'Put a saddlebag under his feet and if there's water, bring me some.' I was surprised to find that my orders were instantly obeyed. Apparently the young man was important to them. He groaned and opened his eyes, black holes in the starlight. In the faint light his face looked like a skull, white skin stretched tight over the angled bones around the orbits.

'I'm all right,' he said, trying to sit up. 'Just a bit dizzy though.' I put a hand on his chest and pushed him flat.

'Lie still,' I ordered. I carried out a rapid inspection by touch, then rose on my knees and turned to a looming shape that I deduced from its size to be the leader, Dougal.

'The musket wound has been bleeding again, and the idiot's been knifed as well. I think it's not serious, but he's lost quite a lot of blood. His shirt is soaked through, but I don't know how much of it is his. He needs rest and quiet; we should camp here at least until morning.' The shape made a negative motion.

'Nay. We're farther than the garrison will venture, but there's still the Watch to be mindful of. We've a good fifteen miles yet to go.' The featureless head tilted back, gauging the movement of the stars.

'Five hours, at the least, and more likely seven. We can stay long enough for ye to stop the bleeding and dress the wound again; no much more than that.'

I set to work, muttering to myself, while Dougal, with a soft word, dispatched one of the other shadows to stand guard with the ponies by the track. The other men relaxed for the moment, drinking from flasks and chatting in low voices. The ferret-faced Murtagh helped me, tearing strips of linen, fetching more water and lifting the patient up to have the dressing tied on, Jamie being strictly forbidden to move himself, despite his grumbling that he was perfectly all right.

'You are not all right, and it's no wonder,' I snapped, venting my fear and irritation. 'What sort of idiot gets himself knifed and doesn't even stop to take care of it? Couldn't you tell how badly you were bleeding? You're lucky you're not dead, tearing around the countryside all night, brawling and fighting and throwing yourself off horses . . . hold still, you bloody fool.' The rayon and linen strips I was working with were irritatingly elusive in the dark. They slipped away, escaping my grasp, like fish darting away into the depths with a mocking flash of white bellies.

Despite the chill, sweat sprang out on my neck. I finally finished tying one end and reached for another, which persisted in slithering away behind the patient's back. 'Come back here, you . . . oh, you goddamned bloody bastard!' Jamie had moved and the original end had come untied.

There was a moment of shocked silence. 'Christ,' said the fat man named Rupert. 'I've ne'er heard a woman use such language in my life.'

'Then ye've ne'er met my Auntie Grisel,' said another voice, to laughter.

'Your husband should tan ye, woman,' said an austere voice from the blackness under a tree. 'St Paul says "Let a woman be silent, and –"'

'You can mind your own bloody business,' I snarled, sweat dripping behind my ears, 'and so can St Paul.' I wiped my forehead with my sleeve. 'Turn him to the left. And if you' – addressing my patient – 'move so much as one single muscle while I'm tying this bandage, I'll throttle you.'

'Och, aye,' he answered meekly.

I pulled too hard on the last bandage, and the entire dressing scooted off.

'Goddamn it all to hell!' I bellowed, striking my hand on the ground in frustration. There was a moment of shocked silence, then, as I fumbled in the dark for the loose ends of the bandages, further comment on my unwomanly language.

'Perhaps we should send her to Ste Anne's abbey, Dougal,' offered one of the blank-faced figures squatting by the road. 'I've not heard Jamie swear once since we left the coast, and he used to have a mouth on him would put a sailor to shame. Four months in a monastery must have had some effect. You do not even take the name of the Lord in vain any more, do ye, lad?'

'You wouldna do so either, if you'd been made to do penance for it by lying for three hours at midnight on the stone floor of a chapel in February, wearing nothin' but your shirt,' answered my patient.

The men all laughed as he continued, 'The penance was only for two hours, but it took another to get myself up off the floor afterwards; I thought my . . . er, I thought I'd frozen to the flags, but it turned out just to be stiffness.'

Apparently he was feeling better. I smiled, despite myself, but spoke firmly nonetheless. 'You be quiet,' I said, 'or I'll hurt you.' He gingerly touched the dressing, and I slapped his hand away.

'Oh, threats, is it?' he asked impudently. 'And after I shared my drink with ye too!'

The flask completed the circle of men. Kneeling down next to me, Dougal tilted it carefully for the patient to drink. The pungent, burnt smell of very raw whisky floated up, and I put a restraining hand on the flask.

'No more spirits,' I said. 'He needs tea, or at worst, water. Not alcohol.'

Dougal pulled the flask from my hand, completely disregarding me, and poured a sizable slug of the hot-smelling liquid down the throat of my patient, making him cough. Waiting only long enough for the man on the ground to catch his breath, he reapplied the flask.

'Stop that!' I reached for the whisky again. 'Do you want him so drunk he can't stand up?'

I was rudely elbowed aside.

'Feisty wee bitch, is she no?' said my patient, sounding amused.

'Tend to your business, woman,' Dougal ordered. 'We've a good way to go yet tonight, and he'll need whatever strength the drink can give him.'

The instant the bandages were tied, the patient tried to sit up. I pushed him flat and put a knee on his chest to keep him there. 'You are *not* to move,' I said fiercely. I grabbed the hem of Dougal's kilt and jerked it roughly, urging him back down on his knees next to me.

'Look at that,' I ordered in my best ward-sister voice. I plopped the sopping mass of the discarded shirt into his hand. He dropped it with an exclamation of disgust.

I took his hand and put it on the patient's

shoulder. 'And look there. He's had a blade of some kind right through the trapezius muscle.'

'A bayonet,' put in the patient helpfully.

'A bayonet!' I exclaimed. 'And why didn't you tell me?'

He shrugged, and stopped short with a mild grunt of pain. 'I felt it go in, but I couldna tell how bad it was; it didna hurt that much.'

'Is it hurting now?'

'It is,' he said shortly.

'Good,' I said, completely provoked. 'You deserve it. Maybe that will teach you to go haring round the countryside kidnapping young women and k-killing people, and . . .' I felt myself ridiculously close to tears and stopped, fighting for control.

Dougal was growing impatient with this conversation. 'Well, can ye keep one foot on each side of the pony, man?'

'He can't go anywhere!' I protested indignantly. 'He ought to be in hospital! Certainly he can't –'

My protests, as usual, went completely ignored.

'Can ye ride?' Dougal repeated.

'Aye, if ye'll take the lassie off my chest and fetch me a clean shirt.'

WHAT IF YOUR FUTURE
WAS THE PAST?

**Continue reading the first book in the
Outlander series**

Available from your local bookshop or online.